SWit'CH On

Write On

Read On...

SWitCH

SWit'CH On, Write On Read On...

A showcase of creativity from
Swinton Writers in t'Critchley House
with All Write on th'Height

CONTENTS

Acknowledgements 3
Introduction 5
Bill Cameron and Barry Seddon

Ageing 8
Anne Winnard

Little Girl Lost 10
Bill Cameron

I am Yours 14
Mary T Connor

Superpower Gogglebox 15
Lillian Hassall

A Night In A Sand Dune..................19
Alan Rick

The Little Mill Girl..........................22
Lillian Hassall

Torn Stockings................................24
Mary Connor

Fred **26**

    By Lillian Hassall

An Unfair World **27**

    Joyce Spalding

Mrs Spider **29**

    By Lillian Hassall

Agony Aunt **30**

    Shaun Kelly

Untold **34**

    John Hassall

Ezekiel **38**

    Barry Seddon

The Never Olympic Star **42**

    By Mavis Crowe

Our Kitchen Walls **44**

    Lesley Hollows

Shock 'n' Roll **46**

    Bill Cameron

Revolution ... 51
By Mavis Crowe

Dead Shot ... 52
Barry Seddon

Prologue - On the Job Philosophy .. 55
Alan Rick

The Grimlaut Family ... 56

My Best Friend ... 61
Mavis Crowe

A Rebel Without a Cause ... 62
Shaun Kelly

The Phone Call ... 65
Anne Winnard

A Lady Called Beth ... 67
By Lillian Hassall

Ugly Old Bat ... 69
Bill Cameron

Coming Home 71
Mavis Crowe

The Pied Piper of Handforth 74
Barry Seddon

Should I Go or Should I Stay? 78
Anne Winnard

One Line in the History Books 81
Joyce Spalding

Beware the Demons of the Night 84
Alan Rick

Grumpy Old Men 85
Lillian Hassall

Cap'n Flint's Story 87
Bill Cameron

Miffy 90
Mavis Crowe

Ill Wind 93
Barry Seddon

Through the Eyes of a Baby 96
Anne Winnard

Abduction 100
Lillian Hassall

A Fading Beauty 103
Lillian Hassall

Rex – The Philosopher King 104
Alan Rick

One Minute 106
Mavis Crowe

Oh Beth Where is thy Sting? 107
Bill Cameron

At Fox Gill House 110
Shaun Kelly

Seasons 114
Lillian Hassall

The Pied Piper of Hamelin – The Rat's Story ... 115

Mavis Crowe

Christmas Bounty ... 117

Lillian Hassall

1066 ... 118

Alan Rick

My Frank ... 121

Barry Seddon

Friendship ... 124

Guest writer Eric MacKinder

Billy Joe and I ... 125

Anne Winnard

The interview ... 129

Alan Rick

Cockle Woman ... 132

Shaun Kelly

Pleasures of Long Ago 136

Mary Connor

Rescue 137

Joyce Spalding

Drifting 138

Barry Seddon

Ode to a Buffoon 141

alan Rick

A Lesson in Life. 142

Alan Rick

Kitchen Calamities 145

SWit'CH ensemble

Other Publications by SWit'CH 153

Copyright and Ordering

Copyright © 2021 by SWit'CH

All rights reserved. This book or any portion thereof may not be reproduced or used in any manner whatsoever without the express written permission of the authors except for the use of brief quotations in a book review or scholarly journal.

First Printing: 2016
ISBN: 9798699906048

Swinton Writers in t'Critchley Hub
Age UK Critchley Community Hub
75 Chorley Road
Swinton
Manchester
M27 4AF
United Kingdom

Web site: http://www.switchwriters.btck.co.uk/

Ordering Information:

Published with Amazon KDP. Available through Amazon and good book distributors or directly from Age UK at the address above or
E-mail: switchswinton@gmail.com

　　All rights reserved.

CONTENTS

ACKNOWLEDGEMENTS

Heartfelt thanks to all who have helped us....

The staff and volunteers at Age UK at Critchley House, particularly Jill of all trades Nichola, brew-maker extraordinaire Mary and John our multi-star chef, whose hot meals and take-homes often save the day.

Copy typist and sometime proof reader, Mary Cameron, who, unflinching and uncomplaining, braves the stormy waters of hand-written manuscripts and still manages to make treats such as a huge birthday cake, enough for all of us (and to spare!).

Our talented artist friends from *Paint Pots and Pencils*, St John's Church, Irlams-o' th'-Height, whose creations grace the pages of this book.

Friends and fellow-writers from our sister-group *All Write On th' Height,* who meet at King Street Library on alternate Saturdays from 10.30 am till noon.

Supportive and appreciative audiences at Age UK, the Humphrey Booth Resource Centre, St Ann's Hospice and Salford Talking News.

Salford CVS for help from the Salford Together Neighbourhood Fund.

And not least, our many family members and friends too numerous to list. They know who they are.

INTRODUCTION

Bill Cameron and Barry Seddon

PEOPLE have always loved a story, since the days when they sat around a fire, enthralled by tales of heroes and lovers. The enchantment continues at 2 pm every Wednesday afternoon in Swinton, near Manchester, when a group of story-lovers read and talk about what they have written since the previous week.

SWit'CH ON The group, started by Swintonian Bill Cameron in March 2015, is called SWit'CH, which stands for **S**winton **W**riters **in t' C**ritchley **H**ouse. They meet in the internet cafe of Age UK at 75 Chorley Road. It is a social gathering, not a classroom. The men and women whose words appear in this book write for pleasure and fun -- stories long and short, scripts, anecdotes, articles, parodies and poems. This showcase of their work is their first anthology.

Much of it is based on challenges and exercises designed not only to stretch the writers, but also to entertain their readers. Subjects vary: often about the writers' own lives, or inspired by subjects ranging from holiday photographs and insects to historical research and anniversaries. There have been visits to places of local interest and inspiration such as Ordsall Hall, with more trips in the pipeline. Members are also encouraged to discover their hidden talents, by trying activities such as editing and proof-reading, where the eagle-eye scrutiny of proof reader Keith Smith is recognized and acclaimed.

Then there is publishing, the proof of which is the book in your hands. The autobiography of one SWit'CH member, published to professional standard, is already on sale. Group members helped with it by reading through the initial manuscript to spot oversights. Artistic talent for the illustrations was supplied by our friends from the art group Paint Pots and Pencils, based at St John's Church, Irlams o' th' Height

WRITE ON SWit'CH is not an exclusive little club whose members read only to each other. They interact with people outside their meeting place. They have visited St Ann's Hospice at

Little Hulton to read to patients, have been to the studio and recorded their stories in The Salford Talking News Magazine and have supplied stories for a local church magazine. To mark their support of Dementia Awareness Week, they have provided readings during a visit to the Humphrey Booth Day Centre in Swinton.

On their Age UK home territory there have been group performances for various local dignitaries, and an unforgettable "double act" by two of the group's members at a meeting of Dementia Support officials. One hapless non-Scottish member, believing that he would only be "reading a story" during a Robert Burns celebration, was tricked into reading the famous dialect-laden *Toast to the Haggis*. He escaped with a not-quite-rapturous ripple of applause -- and his life.

It should be clear by now that SWit'CH does not operate in a vacuum. It works with similar groups such as All Write on th'Height (apostrophes rule OK!) Its constitution promises to encourage everyone from the local community to enjoy every aspect of writing, from recreation to education. Friendly advice and encouragement are on tap -- plus cups of tea and coffee and lots of chat.

The key word is Community. SWit'CH is for all. You will be welcomed at Age UK, Critchley House, 75 Chorley Road, Swinton, any Wednesday at 2 pm.

There is a balanced mix of men and women in the 12-strong group. Like the writers themselves, their writings have a wonderful vim and vigour, show-casing everything from dry humour about army service to science fiction, from private eyes to poems, rebellious teenagers to kitchen disasters and all stops in between.

Our authors are as interesting as the characters in their yarns. They are the writers and (make no mistake) they are very important. But every one of them would agree that the stories are even more important.

Hopefully, you will also agree. Please tell your friends -- and come back for anthology number two!

READ ON...

AGEING

Anne Winnard

Ageing is not much fun
That's true.
It prevents us doing
Things we always liked to do.
Staying up late,
Dancing 'til dawn,
All in the past,
Long ago gone.

Ten o' clock
We begin to flag.
Time to get ready to go up to bed.
But inside our memories
We still remain young
And want to do the same again.

Youngsters think we're decrepit and thick.
"You didn't invent sex, we did."
Ahh, we thought that too
Forgetting our dads and mums in their prime,
They also enjoyed life and love in their time.

We are lucky.
We have Age UK
Where we meet
Say what we want to say.
No discrimination, no inequality.
It opens new doors,
Greets and welcomes us with dignity,
Equal in all we do.
Please come along and join us.
We'd love to have you.

LITTLE GIRL LOST

Bill Cameron

Jimmy had decided that he had to get out of this rut. But it was the third time this week he'd made that decision. And three times a week had been the average for the last eighteen months since he came back up to Manchester. If he was honest with himself the rut was the gutter. The rut became deeper and harder to conquer the longer he deferred so he remained penniless, homeless and hopeless.

As usual, he looked back to four or five years ago, as a nineteen year old lad about town. He left Jenny to make his mark in London. He was getting tired of her uppity airs – "Call me Jennifer now, darling. Open the door for me dearest." He had already decided to move on a good while before she told him she was pregnant. Her family were well-heeled and could look after her better than him anyway, so she wasn't losing anything.

London had been okay for a few years but the crash crushed him and he ran away from London in the same gutless way that he had abandoned Jenny.

So here he was back home, mongrel Jip his only friend, begging for coppers at the posher end of Deansgate. At least in Manchester someone would occasionally stop for a chat but so far no one could offer him work. Consequently he was homeless, collecting no state benefit.

It was a young girl in a party frock who changed his life that day in May. What she was doing alone on the busy streets he couldn't imagine, but she was more than welcome company as she petted and talked to Jip. Somehow this mere animal identified the good in the people who stopped – he growled at the spitters, kickers and cussers who soon moved on.

"What's his name?" she asked.

Jimmy answered, "He's called Jip and keeps me company. Are

you lost?"

"I'm not lost. I'm just looking for my Daddy," she said. "Mummy says he'll probably be in a pub somewhere in town."

Jimmy stood up, gathering his blanket and collecting cup. "Well, I think your Mummy will be looking for you. Let's try to find her, should we?"

She knew as children do, this was a nice man so she took his hand.

"That's a pretty dress. Were you at a party?"

"It was my Aunty Joan's wedding. Everyone was dressed in beautiful clothes and my Mummy put on all her sparkly jewlery, as well. We got there in a big long car. But it wasn't a wedding like normal in a church. So that's strange isn't it?"

Jimmy racked his brain. How would he get this lost girl back safely and where to? Her parents must surely be looking for her.

Then a voice over his shoulder, "I'll take her from here. Save you getting the police involved."

If a voice could be called slimy this was the sinister sound Jimmy heard.

"I don't like that man", the girl whispered as she cowered trembling behind Jimmy's legs – Jip growled.

Jimmy ignored his first instinct for a safe resolution. He wasn't going to say okay and abdicate responsibility for the girl's welfare to the stranger with shifty eyes and sardonic forced smile. With determination he hadn't showed since school, he pushed the stranger away,

"Get lost or I will call the police."

He walked away holding the girl's shaking hand. Jimmy was on top of the world when she smiled at him. New-found belief in himself also activated his brain. A wedding in town, but not a church but it must be nearby. It couldn't be anywhere else but the Register Office in Jacksons Row.

He had spent long years finding his way round town so turned off Deansgate into the maze of quieter alleyways and side streets. In trying to avoid any more confrontation they ran into the exact opposite. As they rounded a corner into a deserted alleyway, they were faced by a group of four youths.

"Hey old man stinky, is that your new girlfriend?" said one.

"No he's a paedo," said another, "and we don't like paedos do we? Shall we sort him out lads?"

The four lined up across the alley, barring their way, each baring his teeth in a cruel sneer.

Ordinarily Jimmy would have run or pulled his hoody over his face and scuttled through the thugs, taking a kick in the shins, a punch in the ribs, spittle and abuse. But now he had this poor child to look after. He pulled himself up to a full six foot. He stared coldly into the eyes of the one he had identified as the leader. He strode forward with purpose.

"Get out of our way if you know what's good for you," the new Jimmy ordered – Jip growled.

The gang stood puzzled for a moment by the unexpected challenge and then parted with feigned bravado, "Go on then, the police will get you anyway."

In the space of a quarter of a mile from his pitch to here, Jimmy felt he had grown another three inches. Confident in himself he decided to "have words with" the irresponsible drunken father when they met.

When they got there he left Jip on the step and took the girl into the registrar's building. They found the wedding party in a sombre mood now that the girl's disappearance had filtered through.

Jimmy asked his new little friend, "Which one's your Daddy?"

She answered, "Silly man! Daddy's not **here**. Mummy said he ran off to the pub before I was even born and never came back."

Then she let out a scream of delight, "Mummy, Mummy, Mummy."

Letting go of Jimmy's hand, the prodigal daughter ran through the crowd. Jimmy's eyes followed her flight. His heart stopped beating, His mind went into a flat spin and his breath choked in his throat. A tear formed in the corner of his eye. Jenny! He wondered if she would recognise him also, in spite of his dishevelled state.

I Am Yours

Mary T Connor

I am the illusion, of feelings to come,

Of fleeting moments, of happiness and fun,

Be it those extra minutes you spend in bed

Or the quiet embrace, where words go unsaid.

Life can be difficult and move at a great pace.

But if you ignore me, I cannot be replaced.

And if I am not managed I am lost for ever

I can never be brought back

Can never be re-arranged

I am yours only,

For this moment in time

I am time.

Superpower Gogglebox

Lillian Hassall

I'm a Superpower Gogglebox
Tom Devorough is my name.
If you answer A, B or C correctly
You might win me as your game.
It took six strapping lads
To load me on their truck,
"Some lucky geezers had a score,"
I heard them say. "What luck!"

They put their little satnav on,
Then pressed a button - GO.
Then gently over the bumps they went
And took it very slow.
I am a delicate cargo,
They wrapped me nice and warm,
They'll be in a lot of trouble
If I come to any harm.

"Err! These streets are very narrow!!"
As they get nearer to the house,
"They're two up two down." They did gasp in horror!!
"This Gogglebox is not a flaming mouse."
Then they reached their destination

And knocked upon the door
"Who is it?" shouts a voice inside,
As he shuffles across the floor.

"It's the delivery men with your compo prize"
As they stare each other out,
"Oh OK then" a tiny voice did shout.

Little heads with curlers in
were popping round their doors,
then sweeping their front paths
And mopping up their floors.
Chains undone and locks unbolted
A little man appeared,
"Thank you very much" he said
"It's the first time ever a prize I've won
in my ninety two year."

In went the men,
They were over six foot tall
They had to bend their heads as
they went, going down the hall.
"Err!! Where do you want your prize to hang?"
They queried with the man,
"Well, just put it on the table,
I'll shift the cups and then you can."

They looked about in amazement
And thought. "What can we do?"
It won't come up the hallway,
It won't come through the door.
"Err! Excuse me mate,
Before we start to bring it in,
Do you mind if we use your loo?"
Then off they went to their big truck
To let the tailgate down,
Then they took a measuring tape and
Measured me up and down.

"Err, excuse me mate, what do we do?"
"It won't fit through your door, or your hallway through."

"Why? The old man said.
The men looked back and did reply
"Cos it's fifty two inches high!"
"Oh!" the old man did cry

"I'll tell you what we'll do,
We'll go back inside and see what we can do."
"You can open up the window,
Whilst I will make a brew."
"We'll chuck out the old table,
And throw the chairs as well.
You can ditch that big old dresser

*And all those pictures too, include
That horsehair sofa and that antique church bell too."*

*Now just leave me my soft armchair and a cushion or two,
A little round table to rest my favourite brew,
Maybe a blanket to keep me nice and warm
Then my walking-stick to keep me from all harm.
Just leave me that old fire
And my photograph of Grace
Take down that big cracked mirror
And put my prize in place.*

*I'll watch a game of football
And er! Question Time, me thinks
Then a nice hot chocolate
And maybe forty winks.
And when I wake I'll chat with Grace
We'll talk about the day I've had
Then show her my prize in place
I know my years say ninety-two, but deep inside
At heart I'm only a lad. "Night, Night Tom Devorough"*

A Night In A Sand Dune

Alan Rick

For some unaccountable reason my fourteen weeks initial training at Aldershot was held to have made me fit for active service abroad in one of Britain's hotspots in the 1950s. The arena in question was Egypt where the Fedayeen, the Egyptian underground movement dedicated to the expelling of the British occupation force from their country was operating in a way that made me feel very uncomfortable.

The year was 1953 and, the King having died the previous year, Princess Elizabeth had just been crowned the new monarch and parties to celebrate the event were being staged in all parts of the Suez Canal zone. Needless to say, manna from heaven, in the shape of barrels of beer were being poured down thirsty soldiers' throats and cries of "God bless you ma'am" rent the desert air at frequent intervals. My own contribution to the general bacchanalia was to imbibe rather more of the lubricant than was wise in a tropical climate.

The time to make my way, with two similarly inebriated friends back to our own camp arrived. We set out, arms around each other's shoulders, to walk across the seemingly unending expanse of the desert in a state of blissful haze. I should mention that in the event of a sandstorm sand dunes of up to six to eight feet in depth are created in the sand and down one of these I suddenly fell and found myself lying on my back looking up at the stars on a cloudless middle-eastern night. My companions, not having any idea where I had gone, had continued on their way without me.

I must have been asleep for some time because when I came to I became conscious of the stern faces of two of the military police peering down at me. This was not a good omen – the redcaps were not noted for their amiable spirit and questions would follow. Rescued from the depths of the dune, I was required to explain my presence in it. This was not possible, as I could remember nothing from the night before. I was asked to produce my paybook. This was the book that had the details of a soldier's identity and it was an offence not to have it on you. I had already committed that offence because my paybook was lost somewhere in the sands of the desert. Establishing my identity was also a problem as the night's revels had addled my powers of recall and in answer to the question "Who are you?" I replied "Napoleon." Military Police are not noted for their sense of humour and I was thrust firmly into their vehicle and driven back to my camp where I promptly fell asleep.

Came the dawn and I was informed that I had been charged with an impressive array of offences and was to parade before the commanding officer at 10.00am.

At the appointed time, I was marched into his office by one of the redcaps – a corporal of particular repellent demeanour – to find the C.O. seated impassively at his desk. He wore a look of world-weary resignation; he was used to erring miscreants appearing before him.

"What is the charge, Corporal?" he enquired in a languid tone. The Corporal read out the charge. "Conduct unbecoming and prejudicial to good order and military discipline in that he;

Was found lying flat out at the bottom of a sand dune under the influence of a substance which appeared to be of an intoxicating nature;

Was not in possession of his paybook, in contravention of Army Council instructions requiring him to carry it at all times;

When, consequently, he was not able to establish his identity and, when asked, replied "Napoleon" which proved to be incorrect, Sir"

This brought a slight elevation to the CO's eyebrows, who asked the Corporal to wait outside as he wished to deal with the case himself, without any witnesses.

Finding ourselves alone, the CO eyed me curiously. It had occurred to him that my surname was a rather unusual one.

"Are you, by any chance, related to Colonel Rick?"

"Yes Sir – he is my father" I replied.

"We served together in Benghazi," the CO continued, "I can't imagine he would be very impressed with this little caper of yours – do you?"

"No Sir" I replied.

"What on earth made you do it?"

This was my chance to exhibit some nobility of spirit – surely the Queen's Coronation would supply justification for a little exuberance.

"Well Sir – we were all drinking the health of the new monarch and wishing her a long reign."

"That is commendable of course" said the CO with a wry smile, "but I hardly think that laid flat out at the bottom of a sand dune would be quite what Her Majesty had in mind".

I murmured my assent and awaited the outcome. Looking at the charge sheet, he pointed out that an entry would have to be made in the space that said "punishment awarded". He wrote in the space "reprimanded" – looked up at me and said "matter dealt with I think".

Nepotism was alive and well…

The Little Mill Girl

Lillian Hassall

Sally was one of 5 children, And her ma and pa?
They're lost to her now, they were separated you see,
No doubt in her young mind - that they may be
In a workhouse, somewhere near, somewhere far.
This moment in time she's nine years old,
'A girl', more obedient are they.
"Her master is a good natured man"
"She's one of the lucky kids" or so she was told.
She works in th' mill twelve long hours a day.
From dawn it begins till late at night.
One shilling a week is her measly pay.
It's damp and it's dark when there's no daylight.
Monday to Saturday is her working time.
She crawls on the floor so dirty and dusty.
Small pieces of threads she collects all the while.
The air is unclean and smelling musty.
Tying yarn together when it came apart.
Shifting large cans of cotton shreds
To the machine for cleaning and combing wool,
Spinning was done with a spinning mule.

No education for this young lass.

Many injuries to her hands and feet.

Not working hard enough, if this was the case

Beatings were frequent for falling asleep

Cruel bosses in charge "Work hard or fear!"

No rights , no dinner breaks for children in mills.

To be late was punishable by a deduction in pay

This child is so pitiful- oh so dear.

In 1833 the first Factory Act was passed.

Maximum nine hours a day for her age

People began to see and to care

That little ones were being treated so unfair

In 1870 the education bill came through.

Full time for all children to go to school

All little ones should be of great value.

Not only in this great country,

all over the world should be the rule.

Should children be classed as slave workers?

TORN STOCKINGS

Mary Connor

Gillian lay there. She knew it was time to get up, she also knew her life had become meticulously organised to the point of ridiculous. Everything was governed by the clock. It had been her way of bringing some routine back into her life. But her good idea soon turned into an obsession. In the past her life had taken her along at a speed she had enjoyed. Only now when her children had grown, her husband departed, did she feel alone. She needed to work. Her love of natural medicines and holistic therapies helped, but she missed people.

Then the postman came, she heard the letter drop and her heart stood still. With trembling fingers she carefully opened it. A smile slowly spread across her face. Unable to fully understand what was happening she sat, clutching the letter close to her as tears of joy ran down her face. Someone was offering her a position. Not just any job, but one she always dreamt of. And she hadn't even been interviewed.

In her mind Gillian went through the events of the day when the interview should have taken place.

'The taxi arrived, traffic was light, I was careful not to smudge my make up or ruffle my hair, and, after putting on the nice new powder blue jacket I had bought, I started my adventure.

'It was on arrival everything went wrong. On entering the lift, a young man with a briefcase caught my stockings and ripped them. The lift was slow and seemed to stop at every floor. I remember I became agitated as time was going on. I must have looked at my watch permanently as did the other young woman beside me. I knew I was going to be late. Then it happened. The lift came to a juddering stop. The electrics failed and we were plunged into total darkness. The woman beside me started to whimper softly. But with each breath she lost a little more control until she could no longer contain herself and cried aloud in fear. I reached for her, her body shook, she buried her head as her arms enfolded me with a strength I couldn't have imagined. I comforted her the best I could

- the training I had received in the past was now coming to fruition. I had been trained to work with people of varying levels of mental problems and phobias. Tenderly I held her as I spoke quietly and evenly, she become a little calmer but was still sobbing and shaking. I was just thankful I could help her.

'But on reflection, I knew my stockings were torn and my mascara smudged. There were probably dark stains on my beautiful new jacket and I had missed the chance of an interview. The clock had beaten me, the time had gone and with it the chance of a lifetime. The lights returned we started to ascend; the woman tried to stand erect, compose herself but failed. I gave her one of my most trusted antidotes, *Dr. Bach's rescue remedy*.

"You should feel better soon," I smiled.

"Thank you so much," and holding out her hand, "Margaret Millington, I have a fear of the dark," she said as a way of an apology.

"Gillian Coats," I replied.

"I'm sorry," said the petite blond girl behind reception when I arrived, "but all interviews have been unavoidably cancelled. We will be in touch in the near future."

'And now here I was clutching a letter offering me the job. It was everything I had ever wanted, managing a small retreat where people could go to switch off and relax. Where there were no clocks, no schedules just working therapeutically with people who had various issues and problems. I was trained for it and understood it. I had also learnt how easy it was to become obsessed. I can help others gain peace of mind, learn how to survive. And I will live without the dominating, tick, tick, tick.

'And the signature at the bottom of the letter giving me my dream job? *Margaret Millington.*

FRED

By Lillian Hassall

Eh! If I hadn't of met Fred
I wouldn't be in this predicament now,
Eh! If I hadn't of got into bed,
One night of passion and look at me now.
I'm near eight months already
And it's kicking like a footballer,
Fred and meself are going steady
I do hope littl'un won't be a squaller.
I had a figure of 38 26 38,
A position in life I worked hard for,
I look like I'm in a right state,
Huge and round, it's much too late now.
Still, I think I love my fella very much,
He treats me like a real nice girl.
I feel I got to tell ya.
He buys me chocolates and such,
And he calls me his little pearl.
It's nine months gone and baby's here.
I sacrificed all for that passionate night
But when I look at him, he's got brown curly hair
He smells of talc and his eyes shine bright.
He's worth every second of them nine months
Them feelings of doubt. Have I done the right thing?
His Dad, my Fred, said to me, 'Let's cherish the moments.'
Then he went and bought me a lovely ring
A year went by. We are a happy family now.
It's blooming quick how time goes by.

An Unfair World

Joyce Spalding

Where did I put it? I had it yesterday, so it couldn't be far. It was all Mum's fault. If we hadn't had that row I would know where I put the damn thing. She had no right to go looking in my blazer pocket and finding that cig packet. I told her they were Jason's but she didn't believe me! She never trusts me -- how brutal is that?

Anyway, I've given up smoking today (no money, no cigs and it was making my breathing a bit funny when I was playing football).

I had no idea where the stupid lead was, but if I didn't take the stupid dog for a stupid walk before Mum came home, she would KILL me! She's so unfair to me, always moaning on about something.

I took off the trouser belt (Mum always buys me school trousers that are just a little bit too big - what's that all about?) and tied it to the dog's collar, desperate times and all that. I figured that if I ran the dog up the hill towards school and then ran him back quickly, that should make him look as if he'd had a good walk.

When I opened the door the dog stared at me with a sneer on his face and refused to budge, so I had to drag him out on his backside until with a growl he got to his feet. I started to run, but the dog didn't fancy that so we slipped and slid all the way to the top of the hill.

The sky was completely white and looked as if it was going to float down on top of us. It should have been snowing, but a teacher at school had said it was too cold for snow. It was really, really, really cold and there was ice everywhere. I was glad when we could turn round and start back down. I was feeling a bit stressed by now, so I was glad it was easier coming down again. Soon we were both running and the dog was breathing heavily. Perfect!

I could see the bus stop at the bottom now, the one outside Tesco Express and there were some girls from school waiting for the number 62 bus. They must have stayed behind at Drama Club. How unlucky was that? One of them was Julie Satterthwaite, the coolest girl in year 9. I really fancied her, she was so beautiful and all the other girls hung around her as if she was the Queen or something.

I couldn't let Julie see me running with this old dog. I needed her to see me walking along with the dog at my heel and as we went past, giving her a cool wave of the hand.

I yanked on the belt and the dog's paws slid from under him and his backside banged into one of my legs as he pulled me over. I rolled over a bit and banged my head as I slid all the rest of the way down. I lay with my eyes closed, thinking oh God, oh God, don't let Julie have seen me, it would be so unfair. I could tell my blazer and pants were torn and as I looked along my legs I saw that my trousers had slid down a bit. Why had I put on my Batman underpants this morning? I started to moan, my head was throbbing as if some maniac was drumming away inside it.

It was then I heard a beautiful soft voice say, "Can I help you? You look as if you've really hurt yourself."

"Julie," I murmured and opened my eyes. She wasn't who I'd expected.

Bending over me was a little old lady with permed hair and a bit of a moustache.

I swivelled my eyes to the right and there were the girls having a right laugh at me and Julie who, I might have mentioned, I really fancied, stared at me with her beautiful blue eyes, opened her shell-pink lips and shouted at me, "Weirdo."

The dog was OK by the way, didn't have a scratch on him. Tosser! Life is so unfair.

Mrs Spider

By Lillian Hassall

Hallo! Mrs Spider, are you home?
You've eaten all your male friends
Now you're all alone.
You wait very patiently for something to call
Sitting and feeling the tremor on your wall
With lightning speed, you run to detect
What's stuck in my web? A juicy insect.
How cruel this world of nature?
How cruel this world of man?
For food inject my insect.
Inject it with my venom
Before it escapes. She wraps it up tightly
That will do for dinner, she thinks, very nicely.
She'll stand and watch until it stops moving
Then approaching her catch she begins eating.
Yum! Yum! That was really tasty
Eating your fill and not wasting
One leg then two - nothing was left
Of this poor unsuspecting insect.

AGONY AUNT

Shaun Kelly

Clara von Lubitch. Not an English name.

A couple of years ago I was turning out a filing cabinet and I came across a few faded folded editions of *The Blandford Trumpet*, long behind me now and my first job.

My hands went to Clara's 'Advice' page almost by themselves. I read through and I experienced yet again that baffled feeling of being in the presence of some kind of genius, but a genius which has no name. A black genius hovering around the edges of words but never quite able, in our dull social mix, to find some final means of expression, or even acceptance.

When I left *The Trumpet* about three years later I never again encountered her name until today.

I sat down and read.

Here it was - seventeen, eighteen separate answers to emotional problems lovingly or tearfully or fearfully sent in by the readers of Blandford and district, condensed by the sub-editors and served up cold for Clara von Lubitch to add the topping. As a career journalist I have covered wars and disasters the world over but, as I read on, I could feel again the sheer embarrassment creeping up my spine, the sense of disbelief that way back in 1968 Clara could take these simple cries for help and turn them one and all into a circus act.

The first letter I read was very typical, a young girl with a classic problem:-

"My boyfriend says he loves me but he is becoming really ill because I do not allow him to be more physical with me if you take my meaning, Miss von Lubitch. What shall I do?"

The standard 1960s reply would certainly have been along the lines of;

"If he really and truly loves you for yourself, dear, then he will certainly understand it is best for both of you to wait until you are properly married."

Clara's reply was very different. Clara's reply was as follows:-

"Dumkopf! Is he the boss or you? What you doing staying with dishonest sheizer like this? Ill - ha-ha. Don't make me laugh. I tell you, screw around if you want - show HIM who is boss!"

The *Trumpet* was my first job in journalism and I was very wet behind the ears. I saw Clara around the *Trumpet* office only infrequently but even I knew Clara von Lubitch spoke exactly as she wrote on the page. Not only was this translation from half-English to the written word remarkable in itself but even at the time I was baffled by how she got away with it. I mean, did 'screwing around' (which she used frequently) have some particular meaning in rural Dorset which had escaped me? The editor of the paper was a real old-fashioned stickler for detail, but Clara's page seemed to be a species of no-go area. She did exactly what she liked.

I read another letter, signed 'Plain Jayne'-

"I am worried that at twenty-eight I am on the shelf (a phrase still much used in the 1960s). I have a man friend who is older than I am and who has been very kind to me but he has never once mentioned marriage. One or two little things recently have led me to suspect he might really be married already. What shall I do, Miss von Lubitch? Should I confront him with my suspicions or should I show patience?"

Clara's reply gave Plain Jayne the full treatment:-

"Tell more, Plain Jayne. What little thing? Like pair panties fall out of overcoat pocket? Like wedding ring in wallet? Like wife and four kid turn up at front door? What things? How can I give advice if you skimp on detail, Plain Jayne? What am I? God above? Look, if he really married, then so what? Enjoy, baby. Be happy, stop whining. See him for deceitful creep he surely is. Plenty more fish in ocean, Plain Jayne, so get out there and look."

For the few times I met her face to face Clara was a hard-faced, viperous woman dressed in black with a heavy Teutonic accent. Around her waist she often wore what looked remarkably like a leather rhino whip. She was a chain-smoker and no member of staff seemed to know where or how she lived outside of office hours. Some unkind souls made jokes about garlic and never looking in mirrors, but most of the staff were dead scared of her and I was myself, I remember.

I closed the filing cabinet and tossed the papers into a cardboard box along with other mementos of a hack's career. With this action - a closure of the account perhaps - my mind arrowed back to the one moment I got anywhere near to what and how she was as a person.

One morning I was *en route* to an interview with a parish councillor. As I passed her office my curiosity got the better of me. I wandered in and I remember I asked her outright if she didn't feel she HURT people sometimes with her replies to readers' letters?

Clara leered up at me, her desk littered with letters and typescript and two full ashtrays. She was slitting open readers' letters with what looked remarkably like a ceremonial dagger from the Waffen S.S. She called me 'New Boy' and she called me that now.

"So, New Boy, you wanna know how journalism work, whether I hurt people? First rule, New Boy, get age right, spell name right, yes? Kind of, find the story. Each person got story, is all, New Boy."

She went on.

"My story? My story, yes? My story is about Canada. You know, during Second War I am in Canada? Yah. The Germans send me to Canada. Good of them, yes?"

She put the knife aside.

"Me? Forty-four. You are, what, twenty maybe? Wanna know where I was April 29, 1945, on my twentieth birthday? I was at place called KZ Dachau, sixteen kilometres from Munich, yes? Wanna know how I get there? By train, New Boy."

"I wasn't pretty like you. I have typhus. I weigh thirty-five kilo and people on train are just bits of people. Mostly dead, in bits,

New Boy. The thing save me I crawl over stinking body so I see sun for last final time. I lie there on ground and American soldier pick me on his back and carry me to hospital. So I live. Brave guy that soldier."

She lit a cigarette from her previous cigarette and as she did so I thought I caught sight of faded numbers on her left forearm.

She puffed a cloud of grey smoke in my general direction and for a brief moment I wasn't there for her.

"Me, I lucky, you know? They send me to Canada, the Germans. Wanna know where Canada is? Auschwitz-Birkenau is where. Is where clothes from dead persons are, to be sent to Germany. Rich place, Canada. You steal there. You steal so you eat. Can live."

Clara von Lubitch looked into my face, not unkindly. Instead of the hard granite look to match the voice there was an amusement, a kind of amused pride at still being alive after this time of ... of what? Of agony I guess. Perhaps to her it was all now a great joke.

Yes. A great joke. Behind her cloud of cigarette smoke Clara von Lubitch was thinking out loud.

"The people who write to me? Does the reply hurt them? Maybe. Maybe we need to see joke, yes? Life just a big joke after all, New Boy. And if you get hurt by joke, you get hurt by joke. Is all."

She began quietly to slit open another envelope with her dagger and I remember I thanked her for my lesson in journalism and I wandered out of her office and out of her life for good.

UNTOLD

John Hassall

Joe remembered how he felt that morning, emerging into the bright Syrian sunshine, his thoughts a tirade of unconnected worrying questions. He shouted to his companion Frank.

Joe   Hey Frank what's all the noise about?

Frank   Hi, Joe. I'd be quick and gather your stuff. We're catching some stray shells from what we think are forward units of Peshmerga. They have obviously mistaken us for elements of Daesh moving out.

Joe   My bags are already packed inside. I'll get them now.

Frank   Grab them quick we're heading north. Come on. Get those size fourteens moving.

As the battered old Toyota pulled out of camp, away from the ever increasing barrage of shells, a feeling of panic was spreading visibly through the crew.

Joe   Frank have you got all the paperwork we need to get us across the border into Turkey?

Frank   I hope so, we've all got UK passports and press passes, not to mention all the news equipment and paraphernalia.

Joe   No. I mean genuine Turkish visas. You know how touchy they are.

Frank   Nothing's going to go wrong. Have I ever let you and the lads down? Trust me.

What seemed an interminable amount of hot tense hours later, through the heat haze they could just make out a tall fence stretching across the horizon. In the middle of this vista stood the imposing structure of the border crossing fifty miles west of Nasuybin in southern Turkey - the gate to safety.

Placed at each side were two tanks and two machine gun carriers, their weapons pointing menacingly in the direction of the press team.

Frank   Hey Bill stop the truck while we rig some sort of white flag, so they won't shoot before they ask any questions.

Bill   Joe grab that old receiver cover. That's white and has ties we can use.

Joe   Got it. Give us two minutes to free it.

That two minutes wasn't long enough as an unseen and unheard 75 mm tank shell turned the truck and its hapless occupants into a blazing memory.

At the lonely and heavily guarded border crossing, another news crew waited for their papers to be processed, irritated by the enforced delay. Steven, the crew's cameraman, was testing the telephoto lens on his Sony high definition camera, his eye pressed gently to the eyepiece, focused on a 4x4, moving at speed towards them. The livery looked familiar - its titanium white paint and twin blue flags of the international press corps.

Suddenly there was a loud explosion, the report from a large calibre weapon - very close by. Re-focusing the camera lens, the still moving vehicle suddenly erupted into a ball of flame. Steve sat back stunned with a feeling of disbelief.

Steve   Mitch, did you see that?
Mitch   I heard the explosion. But what did you see?
Steve   Dave. Did you hear it?
Dave   Sure did. Bloody close. What was it?
Steve   I was running a test on the new camera. I got it all. It's on the screen for you. If you look closely, on the right, you can just see the flash from the Turkish M60 75mm. Two seconds later - BOOM - the press Toyota's gone."
Mitch   Dave. Do we have sat-coms?
Dave   Yes, Mitch. Good signal at the moment.
Mitch   Download that footage sharpish before the border guards realise we're signal active.

Downloading the footage took only seconds, then Steve stowed the camera unit and tripod into the truck's foot locker. Almost immediately the truck door burst open and they were ushered out at the point of a gun, blindfolded and man-handled into a waiting mini bus, which sped off towards Mardin closely followed by their own truck driven by one of the guards.

Two days later the Turkish news agency, Anatolia, filed a report of an incident at an undisclosed border crossing saying:

> *During a skirmish between Kurdish and Turkish forces, two press vehicles were destroyed by Kurdish rocket propelled grenades, 300 yards from the border. Turkish forces later recovered the vehicles but there*

were no survivors. One of the vehicles had just passed through the checkpoint and the details of the crew are as follows. Michael Fallows, Steven Curran and David Webster, a news crew from the UK. The crew of the other vehicle are unknown as fire completely obliterated any evidence of identities and personal belongings.

Our condolences go out to the families of the deceased.

EZEKIEL

Barry Seddon

My Dad was an easy-going man who worked hard on building sites all his life. Despite the harshness of his job, the toughness of the men he worked with, he'd never condemn without cause.

"We all come into this world equal," he used to say. "We should be given an equal chance to do the right thing. And no matter our religion or lack of it, our race or the colour of our skin, if we do the wrong thing and keep on doing it, we should all go into the same big sack for a good shaking up! That's what I've always thought, anyway."

Then he'd light his pipe, have a swig of tea, lean back in the luxury of his hard-won retirement and launch into his favourite tale. It impressed me a lot. So much, in fact, that after he'd passed away, I used my lucky ability to string words together and wrote it down as though it was a story, a fiction.

But it is no fiction really. At its heart, it's true. I've called it Ezekiel. I often tell it, like this...

Ted Sharples did not like black men. If their skin was not white he called them n****s, he called them wogs, he called them rag-heads. He called them words much worse.

There was no excuse for it, but there was a reason. Ted Sharples had a little boy aged eight. He should have been out playing with his mates. Instead he had lain in a hospital, legs in callipers, for almost a year, victim of a crash. He would always have a limp. The man driving the car was not white.

In a way it was not surprising that Ted hit the roof when told that they were sending him a new labourer, only just arrived in England, straight from Jamaica.

It was no use. The boss, old man Johnson, had taken a shine to the new man and though Ted had been his highly regarded foreman for almost ten years, you didn't argue with the man who put the bread on your table.

Ezekiel Smith strolled onto the site at exactly 8 on Monday. Ted was waiting for him. It was a meeting of giants. Ted was a good six-footer. Ezekiel towered over him by a head.

Biting wind whipped across the lorry-cratered ground as they faced off. Ted was muffled to the ears -.thick, collarless shirt, plaster-spattered overalls, a woollen hat and an old duffel coat. Ezekiel wore much less - ragged jeans, a loose lumber-jacket over a thin shirt, and an old pair of gumboots.

He smiled as he drawled in honey-gold tones: "OK boss, tell me where to start and I'm on my way."

For some reason, Ted felt uncomfortable. He repressed a shiver, lit a cigarette, blew smoke in the man's face and jerked a thumb.

"Over there. Ask for Joe. He'll find you plenty to do, n***!" He ejected the last word as though it was a fly that had wandered into his mouth.

Ezekiel's smile remained.

"OK boss," he said and strode away, with all the loose-limbed grace of a black panther.

The men liked him from the start and were soon calling him Zeke. He could shoulder hods piled high with weather-soaked bricks and run up ladders as though they were stairs. Even Ted had to admit that the man could work.

"It's amazing! I don't know how he does it" said Joe, Ted's deputy. "He takes five minute breaks instead of ten and it's not a matter of him keeping up with the men. They're struggling keeping up with him. And now he's asking for overtime. I say give it to him. He's worth ten men."

Ted grimaced. He couldn't sack Zeke for working hard! And then a solution came.

A slow smile spread across his face as he said: "OK Joe, tell him to come in early each day and get the site ready."

"So simple," Ted said to himself. "Let the sod work – 'til he drops."

Zeke must have wanted money badly. He started an hour before the men and worked till the light failed. Every day. He was a dynamo.

Still he smiled. Still he kept that big cat poise. Even standing still, massive hand encircling a mug of tea, he still gave the impression of leashed vitality. Some tremendous power seemed to lie beneath those rippling muscles, untapped, waiting for a chance to show itself.

Ted tried his damnedest to drain that power. Gave him the hardest jobs. Worked him as hard as two men. Tried...and failed.

One day the big cement mixer broke down. Zeke stepped in, armed only with a spade and watched by a circle of admiring men, mixed a huge pile of urgently-needed cement. It took him 20 minutes.

"What's he working for. Is he greedy or what?" said Ted.

Joe shrugged. "No idea boss. He's like a clam about his private life."

It rained hard for two days. The site was a quagmire, a foot-wrenching nightmare of mud and clay. It had just stopped raining when a labourer came running.

"Quick! The big mixer's going down!"

It was too. The ten-foot, two-tonne giant was tilting at a crazy angle, left wheels already up to their hubs in mud.

Ted acted fast, grabbed a plank, leaped down into the mud with two of his men.

They had lifted the monster slightly and others were trying to push more planks under the axles, when Ted's plank snapped.

Triumphantly, the mixer smashed down, pinning Ted's legs beneath it, just firmly enough to prevent him wriggling free. Minute by minute it was sinking deeper. Someone lit a cigarette for him, assured him that the crane was on its way.

But Ted knew it would take another 20 minutes. In another couple of minutes, his legs would be crushed.

He closed his eyes. When he opened them, Zeke had joined the circle of men.

"Come to gloat?" Ted ground the words out.

"No boss, I've come to get you out. Now make room in there."

Squatting, the big man edged backwards under a slightly higher part of the mixer, planted his feet firmly on two planks and put his back to the machine.

The men fell silent as he started to press upwards, urging legs and body to straighten.

Nothing happened. Sweat trickled in fat rivulets down Zeke's face and body, staining his shirt as he strove to save the man he should have hated.

Ted lay and prayed for the first time in his life. And his prayers were answered.

There was a sucking noise as the mud began, reluctantly, to yield up its iron prize. And Zeke's muscles jumped and writhed joyfully as he pushed harder.

Moments later, the men were dragging Ted out. As men crowded round him, Zeke just picked up his spade and smiled, then went back to work.

When they finally sat in the first aid hut, Ted turned wonderingly to Joe.

"Why did he do that for me, of all people?" he whispered.

Joe smiled. "Because he's a good man, boss. And there's something else you should know. I found out that he has a wife and baby in Jamaica. He's working to bring them over. Their little son is poorly and can only be cured over here. He's been in hospital since he was born."

The Never Olympic Star

By Mavis Crowe

Once again five nil to me!
It wasn't my fault I had a sore knee.
I couldn't jump, I couldn't run,
I usually ended flat on my bum.
My hula hoop would slip to my knee
Because it was too big for me.
My legs were long, but that was no good
These bars were made of very strong wood.
My bike would fall with me on top.
I never quite mastered how to make it stop!
I could throw a ball, but it would flop
usually nowhere near the top.
I would hit my top with a good strong spin,
But it would end up in the bottom of the bin.
Sports day would come and I would cry.
Mother would say "All you have to do is try."
Miss Fielding would wait at the school gate.
"Come on now," she'd shout, "We cannot be late!"
With a push in my back and a scowl on her face,
You can at least win one race!"
My bean bag was so heavy
I couldn't throw it up in the air where it should go.
My spoon was flat and my egg would roll.
I couldn't catch it, it rolled down a hole.

My feet were stuck upon the ground
As soon as I heard the whistle sound.
The rope would turn and I would jump
To fall on the floor with a mighty bump.
The ball was hit with a mighty pace.
I managed to catch it using my face.
It hurt so much I began to scream.
None of the kids wanted me on their team.
I could swim but that didn't matter,
As I stood by the pool my teeth would chatter.
The whistle blew, the crowd began to cheer.
I could hear my mother scream,
"Come on. You can do this my dear!"
My stomach turned. I felt sick inside,
But I had to do this to hold onto my pride.
The race was over before I got wet!
I was still trying to get down the first slippery step.
No medals or cups were ever won.
I can tell you it was never much fun.

OUR KITCHEN WALLS

Lesley Hollows

I have very vague memories of our kitchen in the 50s. Now, ask me about our garden and that's a different story as I spent most of every breathing second out there, riding my bike, making mud pies, pushing the dog around in the pram and many more other activities that I'm sure I did, but can't quite remember. The one thing I do remember, however, about the kitchen, of all things, is its walls.

Apparently a few houses away from us lived a man in uniform. I was told he was the captain of a dredger and he'd been sent specially from Holland to work the dredgers on the Manchester Ship Canal, a highly skilled job.

Now I lived in Warrington at the time and often went to watch the ships on the ship canal at Stockton Heath with my dad. What's all this got to do with our kitchen walls? Well, a great deal as a matter of fact;

I remember Dad coming home one night with a huge tin and telling Mum he'd got it for nothing and if it was good enough to paint a battleship with, in this case a dredger, then it was surely good enough for our kitchen. I'll never forget Mum's face, the nearest I've seen is the cat in Shrek when its eyes totally lose their colour and just become two huge discs of blackness. Eagerly Dad managed to detach the lid to reveal a brown, greasy looking liquid under which was a greyish looking skin, and the smell, I'll never forget - so pungent, it made all our eyes water. Mum never swore but I clearly remember her squealing, "Oh, bloody hell Derek!"

Anyway, Dad got his way and we became the owners of a kitchen whose grey/greeny walls proudly boasted a gloss good enough and tough enough for a Manchester Ship Canal dredger. I remember asking Mum about it years later and yes it was still on the walls when she sold the house. It's probably still on them now!

Shock 'n' Roll

Bill Cameron

Saturday night, Vince stands in front of the mirror in the living room and straightens his slim tie. He only had to run the comb through his Brylcreemed DA just once more and he would be on his way.

"Where is it tonight?" a voice from the kitchen.

Vince answered. "I'm taking a bird dancing at the Locarno, Mam. I expect I'll be home for midnight, but don't wait up. Leave the key under the mop bucket if you and Dad want to go to bed."

He was only seventeen and nowhere near getting his own key to the door.

A head full of curlers under a paisley turban appears round the lobby door.

"Don't worry, son, we'll be out tonight ourselves. Dad's taking us to the Legion for a milk stout or two. Don't you want me to iron a shirt or press your hosepipes tonight?" his mother asks.

"They're called drainpipes, Mam, not hosepipes. But no thanks, anyway. I've spent some of the treble chance pools winnings. My new Bri-Nylon shirt and my Terylene slacks don't need any ironing, so Zetters saved you a job as well as paying for the new stuff in the kitchen"

"Now I know why I didn't see a shirt hanging on the rack. Yes. Dad was generous with his share of the syndicate winnings. I'm throwing away the dolly tub and posser and the mangle next. Then I'm buying one of those twin tub washing machines and a radiogram would be nice in the parlour. If there's any money left I'd like to take up the oilcloth like Mrs Henry down the street and get some nice linoleum."

"Oh, is that what she spent their share on? Maybe I'll get a look at the linoleum tonight – it's Maureen who I'm taking out. But, I can't stay talking all night; she'll be waiting for me. See you later

Mam. Tarra Dad," as he pulled the door to.

Maureen was waiting as he walked up her path. "You look fantastic. Ready to rock?" he asked.

She looked even better than she had when he had plucked up courage to ask her out on the bus home from work yesterday. Clearly she had made a great effort with beehive hairdo and a little complementary make-up. She was, he felt, stunning in pink cardigan, blouse and red polka dot skirt, flared out with any number of multi-coloured petticoats – all in the variants of Crimplene or nylon, the new wonder fabric. High heels and nylon stockings and foundations from C & A gave her that look of class and maturity beyond her sixteen years.

"I'm looking forward to it." She smiled self-consciously, "Is it a good band?"

"Of course, they are fussy at the Loc – no rubbish there."

She weighed up his drape coat, drainpipe trousers and crepe soled shoes.

"Are you a Teddy boy?" she asked with a slight nervousness.

"No," he answered with a smile, "My Mam wouldn't let me."

Both teenagers were uneasy on this their first date. He could just detect a faint Yardley Black Rose as they walked to the bus stop - together but apart. They caught the town bus and went upstairs. She took the cigarette from him and leaned towards him nervously as he offered a light and then lit his own.

"Thank you" she said. "Have you been to the Locarno before?"

"I've been here only a couple times, but Jimmy and me usually don't go far from home. Just a game of darts or cards in the Airport Hotel and couple of pints on a Friday."

Their conversation continued in a stilted, embarrassed dialogue during the journey to the dance hall. Neither of the youngsters had had a great deal of experience of intimate contact with the opposite sex. But they only relaxed when they took to the dance floor. Quickly, they established an understanding of the shared movement and common interpretation of the rock and roll rhythms.

Demurely, Maureen suggested they leave the floor when the slow 'smoochers' came on. Jiving together allowed exchange of few occasional words and observations.

"Good band isn't it?"

"Shall we have a sit down?"

"What do you want to drink?"

"Cherry B, please." She had heard the older girls in the office talking about what they drank on dates and it sounded marginally more grown up than Babycham.

At that time the Loc was advertising its refurbishment after years of austerity and dull décor. The synthetic fibre deep pile carpet had been carried through from the edge of the dancefloor making the walk to either of the bars a treat for the feet after an energetic number on the sprung dance floor.

Maureen's father had also been part of the treble chance winning syndicate at Metro's, where Vince was serving his apprenticeship. She had just started work in the offices and often caught the same bus home as Vince. As they sat between dances they talked about how the second dividend win was being spent by each family. Maureen laughed as she told how her mother's pride and joy was the black and white check wall to wall lino that her husband had laid in her kitchen. The new gas cooker with an eye level grill and spark ignition came a poor second.

"I bet that's the only time your Dad did anything in the kitchen." he said.

"That's right. So I guess your Dad's the same as all men? Never seen in the kitchen?" She asked.

As they became more comfortable with each other, their talk had become more relaxed and spontaneous.

"Sorry, Mo, it's a myth that men do nowt and never go in the kitchen. At night, when my Mam's knitting or ironing, he's often in there."

"Doing what, exactly?"

She's prepared to be impressed and thinks her escort's father may be different from other men of his generation.

"Lots," He counts on his fingers. "One, he could be mending his bike; two, he has a last and leather so mends our shoes in the kitchen; three, his dartboard is fixed to the back door and four, that's where he polishes the shoes and five, he uses the kettle to boil the water for a shave and his shaving mirror is on the wall – so you can't say he does nowt in the kitchen."

She rises to the bait, "Yes, but he doesn't do any cooking or cleaning or ironing, does he?"

"Of course not! He's no good at that kind of thing. My Mam's in charge of the domestic stuff. Why have a dog and bark yourself?"

"Well in the future, I think men will have to share the work at home. When I get married, my husband won't get away with sitting in his armchair reading the paper in front of the TV."

She immediately regrets letting part of her private personality show and a pink blush fills her cheeks.

He notices this and realises they may be getting too intimate. He offers her a cigarette to take the gravity out of the conversation. Before she can take one the band strikes up with *Good Golly Miss Molly*. He offers his hand and they glide across the plush carpet and take to the floor again. The night continues with many dances, a few drinks and excited exchanges of optimistic predictions on the world to come in the sixties.

The last waltz is an awkward close shuffle, but not unpleasant to either of them. It was a shared moment of intimacy, which could last only until the band stopped.

They catch the last regular bus service home and arrive at her house at half past eleven. There are lights on when she invites him in for a cup of coffee and meet her parents.

"OK, thanks."

He is glad to accept and she leads him through the back door.

He kicks off his foam-soled beetle crushers. He does not want to risk dirtying her mother's new lino.

The kitchen is in darkness as he stands in his lime green nylon socks on the recently mopped wet floor.

"Wait a minute," he whispers to her.

"Yes?" she breathes in anticipation.

They close together - clumsily in their anxious excitement. Her head tilts backwards. He holds her tenderly.

Their lips meet gently.

All night long, static electricity has been accumulating though synthetic fibre clothing, carpets and furnishings. His feet are earthed on the wet floor. The static discharges with a flash of light and an audible crackle. An electric smell of ozone fills the air. Powerful muscle spasms throw the couple apart across the shiny new kitchen floor.

I still feel that tingle on my lips when I remember that night over fifty years ago as if it was yesterday.

Revolution

By Mavis Crowe

Babies died before they left the womb.

Their poor small bodies starved of food.

Mothers would weep but had to carry on.

To fight the daily battle never knowing where the next meal would come from.

Children would walk from street to street.

Cold, tired, and hungry with no shoes on their feet.

Searching from morn to night.

For scraps of wood the fires.to light.

Waiting outside the baker's shop.

Only being able to stare at the bread, pies and cakes with fruit and berries on top.

Things had to change people had their rights.

They would stand up to the stupid king and fight

The fighting began and many died.

Believing all had the right to live their lives with pride.

DEAD SHOT

Barry Seddon

I was awake, with that instant awareness which is peculiar to an 11-year-old. I'll always remember that morning - the shaft of sunlight so solid you felt you could walk along it; quiet creaking in the oak beams as day-warmth eased their old joints.

Meanwhile, outside, the birds were singing. The only things alive in the whole world seemed to be the birds and me. Was I unique? Was I the only one to feel it? Or was the first day of the summer holidays always like this?

For long sun-blessed moments I lay there, staring at the light-dappled ceiling. Then I remembered. Today was extra-special. Today I would make the catapult. The plan had been there for weeks, living and growing in the fertile soil of my imagination. I could have made it on any Saturday, but normal weekends are over by Monday, while holidays are summer-long. Today was definitely the day. Today I would do it. Today I would make my catapult and become a hunter!

Breakfast lasted an eternity. Mother looked pale without her false made-up face. They used to say I got my sensitivity from her and I would laugh at them. Me? Sensitive? No!

I could not see my father's face. He hid it each morning behind a newspaper, as though it would be somehow incomplete until all the news had been absorbed. He never managed to read everything before he left, so he rarely spoke to me. Thinking back, I can't remember him ever talking to Mother.

But finally they left, Father to weekend duties at the office, Mother on a trip to the shops, which was sure to take all day. What to do? Such a long time since I'd been left alone in the house! I wanted to run shouting through its sterile neatness. But the enforced habits of my young lifetime restrained me and I confined myself to strutting through the rooms -- a hunter-in-the-making......

Kitchen, bathroom, my room and the rest of the "allowed" ones didn't take long. It was Father's study and their bedroom that fascinated me.

The study was brown and cool, still scented with last night's tobacco. Father was always trying to be a writer. A sheet was still in the typewriter. Another love story. Boring. Under a heap of manuscripts in the bottom bureau drawer was a bundle of letters, tied round with ribbon. That looked interesting, but I didn't untie it. I might not have been able to tie the same knot. Onwards...

Nothing of interest in the bedroom with its two single beds, its clinical symmetry, bedside tables, lamps, ashtrays, wardrobes, dressing tables, the beds themselves, all matching each other and precisely placed, as though the room was only half as big and one wall a mirror. Out, out! The day and the catapult awaited.

Lawn-dew sprinkled my toecaps as I walked through the cottage garden to the hedge. Somewhere a blackbird was spilling notes across the air -- sounds like liquid silver, drops of mercury across a sheet of glass.

I dropped to my knees and peered into the privet. My eyes, attuned to the dream, soon found it -- a perfectly angled Y-shaped stem. I stripped it from the parent stem, rubbed soil into the bright scar it had left and was ready for step two.

An urgency possessed me now. With my secret tar-stained old jack-knife I trimmed my trophy to size, stripped the bark and left it in the sun to dry. A bicycle inner-tube I'd salvaged from the dustbin was where I'd hidden it, under some sacks in the garage. I cut two lengths, each half an inch wide, and hid it again.

The tongue of an old shoe, already cut to an oblong with a slot at each end, was in my pocket. I threaded the inner tube ends through the slots, bound them with string, then bound the other ends to the now-dry catapult. Done!

Now I set off, following the dream, into the lane. First shot! Oh, the shivery pleasure of it! The round pebble, firm and smooth, pouched in the leather between finger and thumb, the healthy stretch and resistance of the rubber, the hard pressure of the wood in my other hand.

I let go, and the tin on the fence sat there and laughed at me. I tried hitting a couple of jack-in-the-box rabbits, a squirrel, even a collared dove, but I missed - and missed again. Half a dozen shots later though, I was the master of my weapon, walking through the woods, shooting at branches, trees, thistle heads. Never missing. I laughed aloud as I imagined my parents' image of me - the quiet, sensitive boy, sitting with a book...

Then I saw the thrush, perching unafraid, as thrushes do, on a low-sweeping oak branch. There was already a stone in the catapult. I paused, holding my breath. The thrush saw me and sat unconcerned, head on one side. Perhaps my hand was shaking a bit. Anyway, I missed - and the stupid bird didn't even flutter.

"Oh you've done it now" I muttered. "Just sit still a minute." I drew a couple of deep breaths, let them out slowly and froze in place, not even breathing. Then I took aim, let go, heard the little thud, saw the feathers fly as the bird fluttered down. Got it!

I ran across and looked. It was definitely dead. One glazed eye stared up and a small bead of blood trickled from the corner of its beak.

A fierce pride welled up inside me. "First kill", I said to myself, as I walked back into the sunlight. "First kill!" I said again . "Sensitive! Me? Huh!!"

Odd though -- my voice was just a bit shaky. And why were there tears in my eyes?

PROLOGUE - ON THE JOB PHILOSOPHY.

Alan Rick

Lift up the window pane – one bound and we're in – sorted – Hmm! quite an impressive room – stately in a manner of speaking as you might say – my compliments to the owners' taste in furnishing – I should like to praise him in person, were the circumstances different of course – well philosophising is all very well – rather partial to it myself, but when a man has his job to do he must do his duty in a professional manner – know what I mean? – course some put what they want before their duty, but there you are – that's the trouble with your society today – no standards!

Now what's this on the shelf? – an antique clock – at a guess I'd say French – Louis XVI period – got to be – nice piece – seems a shame to deprive the owner – obviously a man after my own heart – a man of taste and discernment – two kindred spirits me and him. I think I can say I'm taking it into custody for both our protection – well, - some well dodgy characters about these days – can't leave your front door unlocked like in my day or they'll be round for more than a lend of a cup of sugar – know what I mean? – sad innit? – but there you are – my old mum always said – Kevin she'd say – most people have decent standards but you gotta watch out for the bad 'un. Don't be in debt to others – the Lord helps him who helps himself – Always borne that in mind I have – you can't go far wrong then.

The Lady of the house don't appear to match her husbands' aesthetic level. Bright red earring – and a wrist bracelet you could put round the neck of an 'orse. – very expensive though. No, I must say I'm disappointed – jewellery is a subject in which I am fully cognisant and, drawing on my wide experience in these matters, this lady is something of a philistine – an also ran in the gentility stakes – know what I mean?

My boy Jason could learn 'er something about fine gems – nicked the best in 'is time 'as our Jason – done a degree in Psychology while 'e was in the nick – they said a course of studies in the ology field would 'ave him become a fully rounded member of society' – I reckon it has too – he's still doing the nickin' only now he understands why he does it. Wonderful thing education – don't let anyone tell you it ain't worthwhile – done wonders for our Jason. Me and his mum was thinking of putting his name down for one of them posh private schools – Eton and 'Arrow you know – give the boy a chance to mix wiv a better class of criminal – know what I mean?

Still better 'ave it away on me toes sharpish – mustn't overstay me welcome – Courtesy towards others innit – know what I mean?

THE GRIMLAUT FAMILY

An uneasy atmosphere hung over the Grimlaut household. Kevin Grimlaut, a burglar with an impressive array of prison sentences behind him, spiced from time to time with the odd foray into assault and battery, was slumped in a chair, a picture of utter dejection. Beside him was his wife Ada, comforting arm round his shoulder. The problem was young Gary, the offspring of their loins. His father was reputed to be Kevin, although there was some speculation on this point - Ada Grimlaut was known as a sporting woman. She was not pleased with her son. Young Gary had reached the age of 17 and still had not one prison sentence to his credit – the first member of the Grimlaut tribe to shame the family in this way.

"Do you realise wot you 'av done, bringing shame on your family," fumed Ada, "'Ave we not brung you up to 'ave some ambition? To make summink of your life and to show some intraponeurialistic spirit."

"You 'ave mum," intoned Gary glumly.

"An' 'ow do you repay us? By goin' down the job centre an' getting' yourself a job as a clerk in an office!" Ada exclaimed with a look of contempt.

"I don't know what your grandad would say if 'e was still 'ere. Generous to a fault 'e was. 'E give the Wandsworth nick 12 years of his life wivout wanting nuffink in return. 'E 'ad standards your grandad."

Ada pointed to her husband still slumped in the chair.

"Do you know wot you dun to that man?

"E's a broken man. Provided well for you 'e 'as. Nicked the best in 'is time for you. 'Ow's 'e going to face 'is mates down the nick now. 'Ows e going to 'old is 'ead up in their company?"

The gloom deepened over the gathering. This was interrupted after a few minutes by a sharp knock on the door. Jasmine opened the door to a police officer, followed by two constables.

The officer asked, "And who might you be?"

She launched into her reply - rehearsed for the possibility of an audition for X-factor;

"Wot-o there! Jasmine Grimlaut's me name. You've heard abaht me mam and dad an me bruvva Jason. Jason done great in the nick. Got an ology degree when 'e was workin' in the prison library. Well 'e didn't actually study for it but 'e was always a bit light fingered wos our Jason so copped 'old of one and stuck 'is own name on it – brill or wot? Me I'm well chuffed cos I'm gonna be a model in mags an' that. Me agent says I could be a famous celebrity on the tele cos I got a fantastic personality. An' I wanna be famous. Me agent says I got unfulfilled potential – I didn't know what he meant. I just got some pics took for a mag wiv me knickers down but that ain't wot I'm after. That's for them wiv no talent, innit? In fifty years' time I don't want to be remembered just for a bare bum. Did some pics in the nood for a mag – me mam weren't too chuffed, but I told 'er it's artistic innit? 'Ad a go on the catwalk but me agent says I gotta not keep falling over. Some geezer in 'is office cum out wiv an odd remark. He said, 'If she was a light bulb she'd be ony 40 watts.' I didn't know what he meant."

The police team entered the room.

"Which one of you is Kevin Grimlaut?"

The senior Grimlaut was duly pointed out.

"Kevin Horatio Grimlaut," announced the officer. "We have reason to believe that you are in a position to assist us with our enquiries concerning the theft of a dozen laptops from a warehouse belonging to Dixons the retailers."

Grimlaut senior gave himself up with the resigned air of a man for whom the procedure was normal.

The reward of £100 was then handed to young Gary who counted the money eagerly.

"Wot's this?" bawled the father to his son – his face incandescent with rage, "You mean you would actually sink to the level of turning your own father in to the Old Bill?"

As he was escorted from the premises his face suddenly changed from rage to excited joy and pride as he turned to his wife. "No need to worry about the boy now Ada – 'E's going to be alright – 'E's going to be alright."

Six months passed at Her Majesty's Pleasure and Kevin returned to the family hearth. Slumped in his easy chair, Kevin Grimlaut, the head of the Grimlaut clan, pointed to the framed photograph on the mantelpiece and exclaimed;

"There's your life's model – there's your guiding star, the one you should look up to and model yourselves on. 'E was an example to us all – a man who 'ad ambition and made summinck of 'is life."

The photograph he referred to was of old Fred Grimlaut, deceased these ten years and gazing down at them from the mantelpiece – the titan on whom the Grimlaut tribe was now being asked to model itself.

"Your grandad never did nuffink by 'alves – 'e 'ad a 12 year stretch to is name – none of your 3 month short stays like our Jason here".

"'Ow did 'e get 12 year dad?" enquired young Jasmin, wide eyed with wonder.

"Well it's all about the law process wot you wouldn't understand," replied Kevin.

"I would though – I dun great at school – must 'av been clever coz they said I was 'interlectually challenged'."

There were uneasy glances round the room at this and young Gary felt it was time for some repartee.

"I know why they gave you the name Nicholas at school".

"Why?"

"Coz you never wore none".

"Oh! Yeh.. I didn't know wot they meant," said Jasmin with her usual bovine expression.

Kevin felt it was time to take control.

He continued, "It was on account of a bank wot he dun wiv some mates from dahn the scrubs. There was a bit of a protest from the clerk in the bank so grandad dun 'im over the nut wiv the butt end of a shooter. They always went to a bank job tooled up wiv shooters – well you get some funny people tryin' to interfere wiv you so you 'av to be ready to defend yourself – stands to reason dunnit? Commin' to summink when a bloke can't go abaht 'is daily work wivaht some bloke interferin' – undemocratic – innit?

At the trial grandad put up 'is own defence – when asked 'ow come 'is bag contained banknotes to the toon of five 'undred nicker, 'e said 'I quote the Bible in my defence – the Lord 'elps 'im 'oo 'elps 'imself'.

Funny thing though, the judge didn't seem to think it was a very good defence – but there you are – some people don't 'av much imagination. Anyway don't forget your old grandad – always remember, it's the entripenurical spirit wot made our country great – built the Empire an' 'at."

Young Gary wanted to know if his grandad would now be let in heaven because he could quote from the Bible.

Kevin explained, "Oh yer grandad will be in 'eaven allright. Even if the 'Almighty did 'ave 'im locked art, 'e'll 'ave found an open winder round the back and got in when no one was watchin'. Resourceful 'e was."

Raising his can of lager he toasted the portrait, "To my Dad and mentor - Gawd bless 'im."

My Best Friend

Mavis Crowe

She is my best friend.

She is always there beside me.

She has shiny black hair and big sparking eyes.

She knows when I am happy and comforts me when I am sad.

She can be good, mischievous and sometimes very bad.

She smiles when she is happy and cries when she is not.

I know I can always depend on her and she will never let me down.

She is my constant companion and I love her a lot.

Her name is Ruby my beautiful Cocker Spaniel.

A Rebel Without a Cause

Shaun Kelly

For most of his life, in one way or another, my father was connected to hotels.

One of my very earliest memories is holding onto a gold ormolu chair in Gleneagles, the great hotel in Scotland, just after the war, a memory all brown and gold and different somehow.

Dad liked to tell stories at the tea-table. This same table is now at my house in Salford and I wonder sometimes how all five of us in the family got around it. It's so tiny. Just an oval gate-leg table, barely worth notice.

One story he told us was about a middle-aged single man who booked into the hotel at exactly the same time every year and who took a modest rather dull single room on the third floor of the hotel and who brought with him, or had delivered, twenty-four crates of Foxley's Best Brown Ale. Always Foxley's brown ale, always the twenty-four crates.

This man never left his room in his whole two-week stay. He simply consumed the considerable number of bottles of brown ale and at the end of his stay, according to dad, he quietly paid his bill and went through the hotel swing doors and was never seen again until the same time the following year.

We were intrigued with this, or I was.

I imagined him as being perhaps a head cashier in a bank or an accountant in a department store. Once a year - just once a year - he locks the top drawer of his desk and he reminds Miss Perkins, his blowsy secretary, he is about to start his annual holiday and to make quite sure Mister Pryce, the Managing Director, receives this and this batch of figures for the annual accounts.

When dad told us about this man I liked him straight away. I thought of him as some species of a wild man, a natural rebel.

What courage, I thought. He deserves some kind of medal, an award for Drinking Hard in the Face of the Enemy or something.

Fifty weeks of total honest sobriety and then two very solidly-crafted weeks of contemplative solitary drunken riot. I loved it.

What I loved most was dad saying that at the end of his annual holiday he just booked out, went back home to where he came from.

But what kind of a man was he? What did he go back to?

Was he a deeply lonely individual who sustained his whole workaday world by his fantasied ambitions for the twenty-four crates of brown ale just once a year?

No. I imagined him as being a chap made of sterner stuff.

I imagined him as being fully capable of pushing the twenty-four crates of brown ale to the back of his mind as he dictated honest and very dull letters to Miss Perkins.

I imagined him as dressed in a neat trilby hat or even an

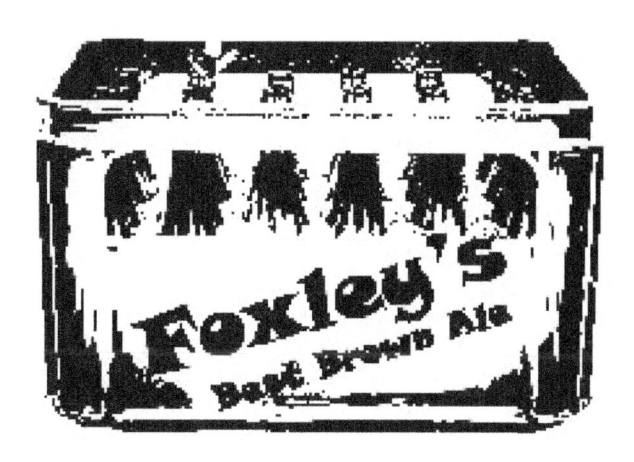

Anthony Eden, with a little moustache and a grey raincoat, who always took the same bus to the same ordinary railway station and who always stepped neatly onto the same train at the same appointed time.

A man who consulted his modest pocket watch encased in his modest dark grey waistcoat pocket, who suffered slight indigestion sometimes and therefore bought exactly the same remedies for this indigestion from exactly the same chemist in the High Street once a fortnight.

A man who was punctual and polite to women and who slept soundly without moving his hands in bed, who occasionally gave money to an animal charity in Sussex and whose mother had passed away only two years before and left him a very small annual legacy, with conditions attached.

I imagined this legacy as being too small indeed to allow permanent release from his neat regular occupation in the accounts office or the bank, so he must struggle on quietly day after day, through that great bulk of days which constitute nearly a whole year. He must struggle on as a neat dull anonymous individual man with a living to earn, a man who must keep going, a man who is doing his duty no matter what, a man who must survive.

But then - once in every year - Gloriana!

Twenty-four crates of Foxley's Best Brown Ale! Approximately three hundred and fifty bottles of glorious, glorious Foxley's!

I loved the man. To me he was some kind of a hero.

A simple man who knew, who absolutely knew without question, that if you wait long enough and if you struggle hard enough then the rewards of Paradise will surely come.

A rebel quite without a cause? I wonder

THE PHONE CALL

Anne Winnard

"Blast that dammed phone," Matt grumbled.

"I'm not going to answer it," he thought.

Eventually it stopped for a while at least. And then off again.

"Hell no. Someone is determined not to allow me to watch the match!"

He stumbled to the house phone, spilling beer from the open can."

"Withheld number. Someone had better not be trying to sell me something," he muttered.

"Who is it? What the hell do you want?" he roared.

"Did you know your wife is having an affair?" asked a trembling, youngish voice.

"Don't know what you're talking about," Matt replied. "I'm not interested. Now just leave me alone. I'm trying to watch a football match!" he shouted slamming the phone down angrily.

The phone rang again two minutes into injury time.

"No way," he retorted. "Get lost!" he screamed. Too late, the answering machine came on.

"I know you're there. Listen to me. Your wife is having an affair. She is going to destroy my family. You've got to stop her," the same voice pleaded.

"Damn," Matt swore. "United has scored and I missed it."

He ran round the room singing, "We are the best, forget the rest!"

He completely ignored the phone call.

"I'll have a couple more beers and watch the highlights of the game," he said to himself. "And then it's off to bed."

Less than twenty minutes later the nagging sound began again.

"You again! What now?"

"Do you know where your wife is right now?" asked in a plaintive voice. "Because I do."

"I'm not bothered." Matt answered distractedly, "She's out with a friend as far as I know. Believe me, my wife has all she needs here. The last thing she needs is an affair with some other man."

"She's not having an affair with another man!" shrieked the voice. "She's having an affair with my mother! Please, you've got to stop them! Help me, please."

A Lady Called Beth

By Lillian Hassall

Stood at the open window,
looking out over the vast garden
My garden, my trees, my grass, my home
A place that I have worked to keep and not discard
This sanctuary to envelop my past life to roam.
I stand in my silky gown, acting out a role to play
A lady of standing, respected in the community
Husband, no knowledge has he of my past life.

Then one day
A letter came by special mail, bitter sweet to my memory.
I hesitated on opening this, half recognising the hand
Of a man I thought I loved, I was but a young fool
I had confided in a priest, Father Ben,
who later became my friend
He listened whilst I shared a tale of misery and ridicule.

Six ladies I had to work with me. A madam I had become,
We signed an oath each one of us a co-operative to start
A few years passed and at last that final day did come,
We divided the spoils between us all and then we did depart.

I gained the strength from I don't know where
To open the letter and read the words before me
I read each line more than once
then took a breath of air.

He'd contacted Father Ben to find out where I'd be.
His life was coming to an end and wandered if I would go
Just to meet him one more time to say good bye.

I pumped up courage and told my husband
my secret of long ago.
He hugged me tight
all will be right there is no need to cry.

We went to meet my lover of many years gone by.
A piece of my heart was with him still.
I introduced my husband no other secret or lie
This part of my life is over now,
I'm still sorry that he is ill.

UGLY OLD BAT

Bill Cameron

Players: Doc   Hypnotherapist

   Patient An agitated paranoid patient

Scene: A Harley Street surgery. Mood music plays softly

   A consultation is in progress. The patient lies on the couch. Hypnotherapist seated alongside with clipboard.

Doc: I want to turn the clock back to before you walked into my surgery this afternoon so we can investigate the source of your neuroses.

Patient: That's why I came to you doctor. A neighbour of mine recommended you, but your patient confidentiality commitment won't allow you to talk to me about the ugly old bat.

Doc   Now close your eyes and count backwards from ten after I stick this relaxing needle in your arm.

Inserts needle and injects patient.

Patient: Ten, Nine, Eight, Szzeven, Zixzzzzz…

Doc: So, you are now sixteen years old, lying in the sun in your back garden – tell me what you see and hear.

Patient: That ugly old bat has stolen my transistor radio. Says I'm playing my music too loud. I'm gonna kill her when I get old.

Doc: Close your eyes again and we'll go further back. You are now eight years old and playing in the street. What's happening?

Patient: I was skipping with my friends and that ugly old bat came out and stole my rope. She said it was breaking her gate where I'd tied it. I'm gonna kill her when I get old.

Doc: Hmm! This is going to be harder than I thought. So now you're eight months old in your pram outside the shops. Tell me what's going on now.

Patient: There's this ugly old bat rocking my pram furiously – she's trying to shake me to bits. She keeps repeating 'Shut up you noisy little brat.' I'm gonna kill her when I get old.

Doc: Let's try regressing further. The year is 1610, who and where are you?

Patient: I'm alone in this massive four-poster bed. Fast asleep in a floor length white nightie. The drapes flutter and a night creature flies in, lands on my heaving bosom. It sinks its evil fangs in my neck and drains my blood and my body loses its colour. That ugly old bat has killed me. I'll have my revenge – if not in this life, then the next.

COMING HOME

Mavis Crowe

It's the early nineteen thirties and I had returned to Worsley Hall to celebrate my twenty first birthday with my dear Uncle George. Uncle George had raised me since my own father, his brother, had died from influenza when I was just four years old. My mother died the day I was born. So Uncle George was the only family I had ever known.

After spending four years at university and then travelling Europe it was now time to settle down and work in the family business.

Uncle George was a rich man owning the local mill. He was a good employer and all his staff held great respect for him. Although he had never marred he was like a father to me.

The only recollection I had of my father was a portrait of him which hung in the great hall. He looked sad with the same empty eyes as my Uncle. There had never been any pictures of my mother as they had all been destroyed in a fire some years ago.

I loved it here at the hall. I loved the gardens and the pleasant walks on the canal banks and the small village nearby. Also the hustle and bustle of the City of Manchester.

It's the night of my twenty first and Uncle had arranged a grand party for me hoping to bring some fun and laughter into the old hall.

Getting myself ready I could hear cars pulling up on the gravel outside, the sound of music was coming from the ballroom where many of my guests were already waiting, I was looking forward to the night but suddenly I had this strange feeling. What it was I did not know.

There was a sound outside my door. As I opened it I could not believe my eyes. There, standing very still, was the most beautiful woman I had ever seen. Her golden hair shone in the light and her eyes sparkled with love. As I stand there taking in her beauty she gently touches her lips with her fingers and places them on mine. Am I dreaming or is this real? I look into her face and she smiles. I feel as though I know her and that I have seen her so many times before. Something distracts me to look away from her - when I turn back she has gone.

The party was a great success. However I spent most of the night searching for the beautiful woman but she was nowhere to be found.

The next morning I woke early, the sun was shining and I felt good but there was something I needed to do. By the window where I liked to work, the picture in my mind was clear and I carried on painting.

After seven days and nights with very little sleep I stood back and looked at the finished portrait I had somehow managed to create. She was beautiful.

Just then there was a knock on my door.

"Come in," I shouted as Uncle George walked through the door.

"What are you doing locking yourself in here? You should be out enjoying yourself not sat in here day after day."

He walked over to the window and looked at my painting. His face went white and tears filled his eyes.

"How did you know? How did you get it so right?"

I didn't understand what he meant. To me it was just a painting of a beautiful woman I had briefly met.

"That is your mother," he said.

He sat down and began telling me the story;

My mother was the daughter of one of the mill managers and her mother and George's mother were good friends. Jessica spent lots of time at the hall with Uncle George and my father.

They had all grown up together, they played in the gardens, walked in the woods picking wild flowers and swimming in the canal on hot summer days.

He carried on telling how his feelings for my mother started to change and he soon realised how much he loved her; how he couldn't wait for her to become old enough to be his wife.

My father was away in the army. On his return it became clear that Jessica loved him and not George. They were soon married and George had to learn to love her from a distance.

That, he said, was the reason he had never married as there could only ever be one woman in his life.

When mother died George wanted to die too. He thought my father also died from a broken heart. The years passed and I myself met and fell in love with my now wife. We had two beautiful children, Jessica and James.

Uncle George had been a father to me and grandfather to my children. Once again I had the urge to paint and I knew I needed to start straight away. My brushes took over. As I carried on I realised it is my Uncle as a young man.

The day I finished my portrait was the day Uncle fell asleep and didn't wake up. George, James and Jessica now all hang together in the great hall. Even on a dull day there seems to be a ray of sun shining on them. If you stand very still you can hear the faint sound of children laughing, birds singing and smell the spring flowers. My father's and Uncle George's eyes now seem to sparkle.

They all look happy and I feel that at last they have all come home and will be together for always.

The Pied Piper of Handforth

Barry Seddon

At school, they gave me a cruel nickname. Hopeless, they called me. Hopeless Henry, always said with a sneer: "Don't ask Hopeless -- he's a right scaredy-cat." In a way, they were right -- I never risked the things a boy usually risks. But it was not because I was frightened. It was to shield Mum from her demons.

You see, I was an only child and Mum was a widow. Dad had died in an awful accident at the flour mill where he worked. Mum had been devastated and had had nightmares ever since, about losing me as well. I stayed within her protective cocoon to save her more grief.

So there I was, seven years old, a quiet boy, small, shy, unjustly branded a 'SISSY'- and soon to face the ultimate test of courage. The result of that test? I'll let you be the judge.

I lived in Handforth, Cheshire, only a village in those days, where lady neighbours were always called Aunty.

I loved animals and one day I was coaxing a baby hedgehog off the lane into the safety of the hedgerow. I suppose I was out of sight of two of my aunties, so I could hear all their gossip about a new teacher, due to join the staff of our church school.

"...and he starts next Monday, if you please!"

"Never!"

"Oh yes, that nice young curate told me, so it must be true. But I still don't think it's right. Why take on a chap from Alderley Edge of all places? They say that Godforsaken place is haunted, you know..."

"And what about young Betty our own local girl? Poor lass! She'd set her heart on the job, after passing all those exams. Anyway, why take on a man? And what's his name?"

"Martin Piper, the curate told me. He also said that, for some reason, the kids at the other school thought he was wonderful. Don't know much more about him. Oh and he's supposed to be very good at playing, what is it? Oh...the flute, the tin whistle, or something. Quite your musical wizard, in fact. He'd better be good at sums and spelling!"

Her voice lowered, "They SAY he left under a bit of a cloud. Seems they promised him a rise then didn't pay him. He took some sort of revenge - don't ask me what - and they sacked him. And now we're saddled with him. He's too soft, our vicar."

The gossipy voices faded as Aunty Maud and Aunty Jane walked on down the lane.

First class on Monday; boys larking about to impress the girls, girls giggling out of nervousness. A man! We'd always had lady teachers. We were beside ourselves with curiosity.

Then in he strode....tall, almost thin, with rather long blond curls, a velvet jacket, cherry-red with yellow piping round the lapels, black and white check trousers and the most amazing shoes, shiny and black, with upward curving toes, just like Ali Baba's. You almost expected to see little bells hanging from the points.

The girls giggled and whispered, the lads laughed out loud and Mr Piper stood silently, hands on hips, laughter-wrinkled, a quirky little smile on his lips, bright blue eyes gazing back at us.

Gradually, the room fell silent and our new teacher (and as it turned out, our new friend) finally spoke. "Good morning children. I think it's a fine day to learn and be happy. Perhaps we should have our first lesson out on the grass. Do you think that's a good idea?"

The girls swooned, the boys whooped and out we filed, to sit in a circle on the summer lawn. The school's two elderly lady teachers peered out at us, all agog, as Mr Piper launched into his first lesson. I shall never forget it. It was all about the things around us and it opened our eyes to wonders...

The way the bees eased open the little lupin flowers to sip the nectar through their hollow tongues; the reason the blackbirds stamped their feet to imitate the sound of rain, then tipped their heads to listen for the rising worms.

We sampled sweet tastes -- of the tender new leaves at the end of hawthorn twigs and of the fat little ends of clover flowers when you pulled them apart..... We were learning. we were relishing learning. We were entranced.

We counted the petals on daisies, then multiplied to find how many there were in a bunch.

Why is the stream just there? Well, look at the way the land slopes.

Why do the tops of those clouds look as though they're smoking? What does that tell you about the wind?

Hear those grasshoppers? There's a way to tell how warm it is by counting that scraping sound they make. And why does it sound like that? Let me show you.

On and on! Crack your knuckles. What you hear is tiny thunder! Shall I tell you how? And did you know you can tell the miles to a storm by counting the seconds between the lightning and the thunder?

The children in the other classes envied us. We were partaking of magic. Little did we know...

Two months on, the magic began to fray at the edges. Mr Piper was seen having long serious talks with the headmaster. There were angry voices, mentions of money, unpaid wages, even rumours of court action.

Then one Monday morning at assembly, after the final hymn, the headmaster announced that Mr Piper was leaving. His unusual teaching methods did not fit in with Church tradition, he declared. Some silly old folk had even been whispering about witchcraft - and we couldn't have that now, could we, children?

Anyway, Mr Piper would leave at the end of the week. Groaning our disappointment, we filed out. The days dragged by, until Friday dawned, as bright as anyone could recall.

Then Mr Piper, who had been as subdued as any of us, stepped into the classroom, smiling and jaunty -- carrying his shining silver whistle.

"Come children," he said. "Don't let us depart in sadness! Let's dance away the day! Let us step lively through the village! Tell your friends! Let the whole school dance!"

And soon, despite protests from teachers and headmaster, we gathered by the gates -- fifty-strong. Then we followed our beloved teacher. Followed his cheeky-angled tin whistle piping its hypnotic tunes, as melodious as the finest thrush. Followed him, dancing, through the village. Followed him, singing and laughing. Until we came to the river. No bridge - just a wide expanse of swirling water.

I expected that we would turn round and dance back to the school, but no! Mr Piper, our Mr Piper, our very own black and white Pied Piper, our man of magic, stepped into the water! Or rather ONTO it.

"Come children, don't be afraid. See, I walk on hidden stepping stones! I placed them here by moonlight while you were all asleep. Come!"

He held out his hand to little Mavis Lamb and led her across. The boys could not be shamed by a mere girl! They followed - and so did the rest of the girls, till all were on the other side.

All, that is, except me. "Come Henry, join us, step out, don't be afraid," called Mr Piper.

I stood still. Could I dare to step across on hidden stones? The moment to show my courage had come. But as the laughing children held hands and trooped off with him, towards his promised land of honey in the woods across the field, I turned and walked away, towards home.

This, I realised, was what it meant to be brave! To stand alone despite the scorn of others. To think of your mother and her grief if you went away.

This was my big test.

I began to run.

Should I Go or Should I Stay?

Anne Winnard

I was not a fan of social network sites. Occasionally I signed in to see what the world was up to. Boring!!! Who gives a damn what you had for breakfast, lunch or tea? More boring still was hearing about individuals' bowel habits.

I didn't attract friends in reality or online, but today I read a notification that stirred my interest.

SITTAFORD HIGH SCHOOL IS HOLDING

A TEN YEAR REUNION.

VENUE: THE DOG AND HOUNDS

ON THE LAST FRIDAY IN MARCH, FROM 19.00 HOURS

I had made a couple of friends during my time at school, but lost contact when I left the town.

This was something of a dilemma. Should I go? Who would remember me or find me interesting?

I dressed carefully, but casually. I even went as far as to have a professional haircut. I left my one-bed apartment at 18.45. My plan was to call in The Pig and Cow for a swift pint. I hadn't intended having two whisky chasers, but they upped my courage. I nervously lit a cigarette on my way to the reunion. Smoking was no longer a habit but I believed it eased my anxiety.

The room was packed to capacity, chattering groups surrounded me giving me a feeling of isolation.

"Would you like a name tag?" asked a small, dark haired girl. She was much younger than I.

I wrote my name on the self-adhesive sticker and made my way to the bar.

This time I ordered a double whisky. "I'll have this and then I am off." I thought.

The alcohol began to take effect.

I was ready to leave. Then I saw her. Should I go? Should I stay?

I couldn't remember her name. She was two years below me in school.

They used to tease her and some called her The Giraffe. She was tall and had mild acne, spots that cause so much teenage angst.

She was known to her genuine friends as Bouncy Bella. So popular, she would bounce back to order and do whatever was required from her, always eager to please.

I think I was probably a little bit envious of her. Because of the two years age difference I couldn't approach her. Two years difference at 28 and 26 was negligible.

I returned to the bar ensuring that I passed her and checked out her name. "Ah yes. Isabella."

She was beauty personified. Her smooth swan-like neck held a head full of long blond hair. She was tall, slim and elegant.

I managed another double whisky and finally found the courage to confront her.

"Ermm hello," I stammered. "I… I don't expect you remember me?"

"Of course I do. You are Oliver Mason's older brother Alex. How is he? I heard he had migrated to Australia," she replied.

"I don't know about that. We don't keep in touch," I said. That was a deliberate lie. I was in frequent contact with Ollie. It was so annoying that he was the reason folk recognised me. I felt an enormous pang of sibling jealousy fused with some self-loathing.

"Can I get you a drink?" I asked.

"Certainly. A red wine please."

I hurried to the bar and ordered another double whisky, that I necked in one, and two glasses of wine.

As I unsteadily approached the gorgeous Bella, my toe caught on a table leg. I was sprawled flat at her feet. The wine spilled over her white silk blouse.

There was no doubt in my mind, I should go!

I jumped up and hot-footed it out of the pub. Idiot!!!

Saturday, I suffered the worst hangover ever. I hid under the quilt trying to forget my stupidity, caused by alcoholic over indulgence. The nightmare would not go away.

Late afternoon my phone beeped, alerting me to read messages.

The message gave me a phone number contact, and a text saying,"Good job you got the wine order wrong. You brought white wine not red, ha ha! Love Isabella. PS I fancied you in school, but you never noticed me!"

I called the number and we arranged to meet the following week.

Should I stay or should I go?

ONE LINE IN THE HISTORY BOOKS

Joyce Spalding

Calpurnia awoke; sweat pouring from her, her heart thumping in her chest. She had had a nightmare and although the details were fading fast it had left her with a feeling of dread, a sense of pain and loss. She scrambled out of bed shouting for her maid, who scurried in, a startled expression on her face.

"Where is your master?" asked Calpurnia.

"He's already with his clients, mistress, ready to leave the house."

"Get him now. Tell him I need to see him urgently."

As the girl hurried away Calpurnia pulled on her discarded robe and took deep breaths to steady herself.

At the sound of approaching footsteps she stood quite still determined to appear calm, but as soon as she saw him her resolve vanished. She ran to him and buried her face in his clothing, breathing in the scent of him, feeling the reassuring strength of his body.

"What on earth is the matter?" he asked, "This isn't like you Calpurnia to summon me away from my business."

"Don't go, Gaius Julius", she wept, "Don't go to the Senate meeting today. Stay here with me; send a message that you are ill. Stay here where it's safe. Stay with me."

He looked at her strangely.

"Calpurnia, you are the most sensible woman I know. What's happened to put you in this state?"

"I had a terrible dream, a message from the gods warning of danger. You're leaving Rome in three days. What does it matter if you miss the meeting? Stay here with me. Summon people here if you must see them, but don't go out. I'm begging you. Messages from the gods should not be ignored!"

He pushed her gently away and studied her face, blotched and stained with tears.

After a moment he said in a calm, soothing voice, "Very well my dear I shall do as you ask. You dress and compose yourself whilst I send away my well-wishers and when the house is empty I shall send a slave to Pompey's Theatre to say I cannot attend today."

As he went away she felt weak with relief that he had listened, not dismissed her as a superstitious, hysterical woman. She called for her maid and, as she was washed and dressed, her hair brushed and pinned, she thought about how happy this marriage had turned out for her. She knew about his mistress and his many fleeting affairs, all of Rome knew, but none of it mattered, to her he was always kind and generous. And what more could a woman of her station ask? She would like a child but he was never in Rome long enough to be sure of getting her pregnant. Despite that sorrow she had a good life with him, a safe life. She shivered suddenly.

The maid asked, "What's wrong mistress?"

"Nothing," she replied - but inside a silent voice whispered "everything."

If anything happened to him her life might become very bleak. She was still young. Her family would marry her off quickly to gain political advantage and another husband might not be as considerate and gentle as he was. There were far worse fates than to be married to him she thought. Thank the gods he listened to my warning.

When she was finished off to her maid's satisfaction, she hurried to find him and ask how he was going to spend the day. She wandered from room to room growing steadily more anxious, the knot of fear in her stomach getting stronger and stronger, until at last she went to the alcove where the door slave waited patiently.

"Has your master left the house?" she asked.

"Yes mistress, about an hour ago."

"Was anyone with him?"

"Decimus Brutus mistress. The master told him he wasn't going out today Said he was just about to send a boy to the Senate with a message."

He leaned forward, delighted to have a piece of gossip to pass on.

"Brutus persuaded him to go to the meeting. Said it was best not to leave any unfinished business, especially if he was thinking of leaving Antony in charge while he was away. Remember how he put up the backs of all those important people, mistress. So the master said he'd better go after all."

"What is it mistress? What's wrong?" he asked as she sank slowly to the floor and crouched silently on the cold marble.

Terrified slaves came running at the cries of the doorkeeper shouting for help. They pleaded with her to move but she stayed where she was, oblivious to the rising tide of noise outside in the Forum - until the lifeless body of Caesar was carried into the house.

Beware the Demons of the Night

Alan Rick

The church yard; a haven of peace and calm. Darkness spreads her cosy cover over all and gravestones stand to attention like sentry guards over the long departed souls beneath them. It is Autumn, and the fallen leaves rustle and moulder quietly on the ground. The moon, like a phantom ship, seems to meander through the sky keeping watch on the graves, as if the gravestones are not being vigilant enough.

Suddenly I sense an atmospheric change; is this calm about to be disturbed? The air becomes cold and I am frozen to the spot as if seized by some invisible icy hand at my throat. The gentle breeze is transformed into a howling wind that shakes the branches of the trees; like a furious cyclone, it screams through the trees, whipping branches into a frenzy and scattering the leaves on the ground into a manic whirling dance. Then the tolling of the church bell with its metallic clang heralds midnight and summons forces whose terror I can feel but whose source I do not understand. The air turns even colder, the leaves more agitated and suddenly from the cavernous depths of the cold earth, spring a host of black clad figures, skeletons and grotesque parodies of humans with emaciated faces, to join the leaves in the macabre rite.

They turn their hollow eyes and sickly stare upon me; the air resounds with their shrieks and demonic mocking laughter. The bats in the bell tower, alarmed by these ghoulish sights, join the figures in a frenzied *round* dance that turns the church yard into a scene from Hades.

Comes the dawn, invoked by the rising of the sun, the moon, as if deprived of an enjoyable sight, sinks slowly and sulkily below the horizon. The dread forms vanish into their stone resting place below the earth.

In the silence a distant crowing of a cockerel signals the return of peace and calm. The bell tower clock chimes; no longer an ominous warning sound, but a sonorous comforting sound to reassure the village people that all is now normal in the day ahead. It is the final victory of the benign over the profane.

GRUMPY OLD MEN

Lillian Hassall

People watching is a pastime I employ
Body language may tell certain things about a few
I'm only a novice, but I do enjoy
Noticing my fellow humans and what they do.

Our faces could tell a tale of how we feel
Anger, joy, worry, happiness or stress
Heads bent low shows an ordeal
Lack of confidence, deep in thought, of sadness.

In Waterstones' cafe I sat reading my book
A heated discussion was filling the air
On raising my head I just happened to look
Grumpy old gentlemen, a very irate pair.

They were shouting the odds about a woman
Apparently she liked one and loved the other
The confusion was that neither of these grumpy old men
Could figure out who she liked and who was her lover

Looking around I was interested to see
Some people smiling, some people staring,
glancing up from their papers across from me
looking back at their news, not really caring.

Fingers pointed, the other with arms folded
Determination was the order of the day
It was sad to observe the two being scolded
And to have observers watching the play.

A lady in red uniform appeared
With concern written all over her face
In her office she had overheard
The kerfuffle, this really was not the place.

She asked the gentlemen to have some thought
And explained to them, not in Waterstone's cafe
It was not right to argue and they ought
To have their discussion another day.

All went quiet, they sipped their tea
Chatter and reading resumed in the cafe
I glanced back at my book, had another coffee
We are all funny in our own little way.

Back in their corner they pondered their problem
Was it the woman that was the bother?
She had dealt very skilfully with both men,
Manipulating one against the other.

When I glanced their way again
They had sorted the quandary very well
Laughing and chatting once again
They were chasing her off like a bat out of hell.

Cap'n Flint's Story

Bill Cameron

I felt sorry for the youth as he approached our table in The Admiral Benbow. He could not have been more than 12 or 13 and hardly started shaving, but my master Sken-eyed Sven Jonssen didn't discriminate on any grounds, young, old, black, white or yellow, man or woman – he would beat up anybody just because he could. Jonssen threw a peanut into my cup to prompt my trained response;

"Buzz off! Buzz off or fight!"

(*ed: toned down for delicate ears*)

My oft repeated challenge - in truth, the only phrase I had ever been taught - was aimed at the lad.

The youngster came closer to the table and asked in a tremulous voice not quite broken,

"May I borrow one of these chairs, Sir?"

Another peanut in my pot and, "Buzz Off or Fight!"

The lad's puzzled expression turned to fear as my master stood, towering his six foot four frame over him with a glare that would curdle fresh milk. His blackened teeth clamped in an angry sneer; the veins on his temple stood like purple vines on his furrowed forehead and his spittle-fuelled roar rocked the Admiral to its foundations. His hammerhead fists crashed into the unprepared youngster, flooring him in a cruel instant.

The nautical complement of the pub was shocked into silence, but not a soul moved to protest against the bullying Swede's cowardly deed.

From the silence at the far end of the room came, at first low, a repeated thud, thump, thud, thump, thud, thump on the bare floor boards. A hunched old man, supported by a crutch under one arm and a wooden leg from the knee down, shambled across the sawdust floor between the stools and tables.

Thud, thump, thud, thump, thud, thump – he approached our table and the violent scene.

"'Ee be a'right shipmate?" he addressed the boy.

No reply from the prone figure spread-eagled on the floor.

But – a peanut rattled into my tin.

"Buzz off or fight!" I addressed my surrogate challenge to the crippled old sea dog.

I don't think a man in the pub followed the flight of the crutch as it first shot in the air then landed firmly in the middle of the scabby bald dome of Sken-eyed Sven – certainly the bully himself could not avoid the blow and crumpled in a heap on the sawdust – never to trouble man nor beast again. As he hit the floor, his palm opened and a fragment of paper fell from it, revealing the mark of the pirates' nemesis - the *black spot*.

"…and I'll take this to compensate young Jim," the old sea dog said as he swept up Jonssen's last doubloons. "…and this chatty bird for company."

He grabbed my legs and firmly planting me on his shoulder. I made no attempt at escape – this had to be an improvement in my life.

I found out later that the old matelot was famous along the Barbary Coast - and every port or harbour on earth - as a rogue and scoundrel, so this concern for the lad and me was a surprise to all.

"Old Long John is getting soft in his dotage," announced the bo'sun of the Hispaniola. "It looks like he may be less trouble as a cook this voyage than he ever was as a deck hand.

I got used to Long John's peculiar ways as the ship was made ready for the voyage and enjoyed decorating his shoulders more than I had my previous owner's. We became inseparable during the days victualing and recruiting a crew and Long John had a large say in choosing both. The diet of a ship's cook's pet was more imaginative than I'd ever enjoyed before.

Young Jim Hawkins also recovered and proved an eager and hard-working cabin boy to Squire Trelawney when we left

Portsmouth. Long John seemed to have a lot of sway with the crew, particularly odd as his status was no more than cook. None of the officers found this strange at the time, an oversight that was to cost them dearly

In deference to the delicate years of the cabin boy, the squire insisted that Long John retrain me to clean up my language and during our days at sea "Buzz off or fight" became "Pieces of Eight", an obscure expression which meant nothing to anyone. The longer we spent at sea, the more my diet included increasing quantities of fish with indigestible scales. It was not too long before the undigested silver scales were streaking the back of Long John's duffle coat. It was a lot later when he understood the origin of the soubriquet Long John Silver.

Eventually, we arrived at the tropical island shown on no other map than the one which was locked securely in the cabin of Captain Smollett.

We dropped anchor in an avian heaven. I had never seen such a wealth of glorious coloured birds - parrots, parakeets, birds of paradise a delight to the eyes of one like me who had spent most of his life in dingy bars and on a sailor's shoulder in a man o' war's cabin.

"This'll do for me," I thought as I spread my wings and took off to leave these humans to their own adventure.

MIFFY

Mavis Crowe

Hello, my name is Miffy. I suppose you think this is a strange name for a dog but I love it, Most of the dogs around here have names like Buster, Growler or Butch.

When I was born my mother had four other puppies and I was the last to be born. I was thin and puny and I suppose I let my brothers and sister pick on me. There was never enough food to go round so I was the one left with the last drops of milk hardly enough to help me grow.

My mother's master, Split Lip Ken, was a cruel man. He wanted his dogs to grow big, strong and aggressive. Of course looking at me it was clear I would never be any of these things.

One dark night in November, Ken took me to a quiet place by the canal and left me.

I was cold, hungry and frightened. Just when I was about to give up I heard the sound of children.

"Come on lads don't be afraid of the dark and fog."

I let out a small whimper and in dog talk said "Please, will someone help me?"

Just then two small grubby hands lifted me.

"Look lads what I have found."

He picked me up and put me under his ragged hole-filled jumper. I could feel the warmth from his body I knew then I would always love and be faithful to my beautiful Mattie.

The kitchen in Myrtle Grove was warm and I felt safe. Mattie reached into his jumper and pulled me out.

"What's that?" his mother cried, "Get that flee-bitten mutt out of my kitchen. Don't you think I have enough mouths to feed with you and your two brothers?"

"Please Mam," Mattie cried, "Let me keep him. I promise I will look after him and share my food with him. Please let him stay."

And I did. I was always scruffy and thin but one thing I had was love from Mattie. He went to school and I would sit outside the school gates and wait for the bell to ring at three o'clock. We would walk home, play in the park or run by the river.

Mattie left school and went to work at Fletcher's Foundry. I went to work with him each day and would sit outside the foundry gates until dinnertime when he would come and pat me on the head, and share his dripping butty with me, pouring some of his cold sweet tea in an old can for me to drink.

Oh how I loved my master.

One day things seemed different. Mattie didn't go to work and there was great commotion in the street. Mothers, wives, sisters and sweethearts lined the street waving flags I could hear a band playing and then all the men appeared marching to the band.

The people cheered and shouted.

"GOOD LUCK LADS. LOOK AFTER YOURSELVES. KEEP YOUR HEADS DOWN. COME HOME SAFE. WATCH OUT FOR THOSE FOREIGN WOMEN. WE LOVE YOU."

What was going on I didn't understand.

The men marched on smiling with their heads held high looking forward to the adventure which lay ahead of them.

To my horror there was my Mattie. What was he doing? Where was he going without me?

The sound of the band faded and the men disappeared.

Time passed.

But Mattie didn't come home.

I would go to the school and wait for the bell to ring but Mattie never came out. I would go to the factory gates but Mattie didn't come out - just tired, frightened, yellow-faced women. Fletcher's was now a munitions factory.

Mary would feed me scraps but she hardly had enough food for herself.

When I was really hungry I would sit outside Mr. Jones the butcher. He would throw me the odd small bone or a scrap of meat or sometimes an old sausage - green with age, but I would eat it anyway.

I would sit on the step day after day just waiting. I got used to see the boy on his bike knocking on doors handing out small brown envelopes. Then the crying could be heard from inside.

One day the boy knocked on our door. Mary could be heard sobbing. She sat at the kitchen table and cried for two days. Just a week later the boy came again.

"NO, NO," screamed Mary, "Another of my poor boys gone. When will it all end?"

I carried on, thinking I would never see my Mattie again. I could only dream of playing in the park chasing the stick Mattie would have thrown for me.

Then something seemed to be happening. The women in the street were out stoning their steps and washing the windows. The few men who were left were stringing bunting from one lamppost to another.

I could hear the sound I remembered.

IT WAS THE BAND.

Round the corner a handful of tired, thin, frightened men appeared. They didn't look like the same young men who had marched off so full of hope.

Then I saw him. Was it really him? Was it my Mattie?

I looked and looked and then I heard his whistle. YES, YES, it was him.

I ran as fast as my poor old legs would carry me and jumped into his arms. I licked the tears falling down his face.

"OH MIFF IT'S SO GOOD TO SEE YOU. I PROMISE I WILL NEVER, EVER LEAVE YOU AGAIN," he cried.

He reached into his kit bag and pulled out the biggest, juiciest marrow bone I had ever seen.

This surely had been the happiest day of my life.

Ill Wind

Barry Seddon

Another boring day on *Paradise Island* thought George Wilson. He had to keep it to himself though, because Emma was over the moon about it. Had been, from the day that smarmy bloke at the travel agents had shown them the brochure.

"Oh George, look at this! Real thatch! This nice young man says you can even help them to repair it when it's been a bit windy. And don't you think these little piccaninnies are cute?"

Mucky urchins! George had thought. Only thing going for this holiday was their lovely white hotel, standing so proud above the weather-worn native shacks. And it wasn't thatch, just layers of long leaves, cut off their shabby excuses for trees.

Thank God there was a bar! Ground floor, and serve-yourself today, but you couldn't have everything. Their apartment was on the 12th floor and with all those hours of sunshine it was a relief to come down. He leaned back against the bar, beer belly bulging comfortably against his Hawaiian shorts, watching the scene outside.

There were always lots of dogs in the village square. Usually they just lay in the dust, panting, tongues lolling. Not today. They were prowling like a pack of wolves, legs stiff, tails tucked down, stopping now and then to sniff the breeze.

That was picking up a bit, rustling the rooftop leaves. But apart from that and the occasional whine from a dog, it was rather quiet. Quite nice really, thought George. He could do without the islanders with their noisy buying and selling and gossiping. Jabbering aborigines. Jabberiginees! That was a good one! He'd try that on the lads in the vault.

Emma could go by herself next time ... and speak of the devil, here she came, dress much too short, that silly big-brimmed hat and that stupid little parasol. Thought it all made her look a la mode! Fat chance...

And she was still gushing: "It's SO exciting George! The

natives are having their annual procession to the top of Waikuto Hill to pray to the weather god. They said they don't usually take strangers, so it's an honour. Quite cheap too. Are you coming?"

She named a figure that made George's eyes water, so he was quite sincere when he said that no, he'd see her tonight when she got back. And off she floated, with the chieftain and all the dusty village folk and their kids

An hour after they'd gone, the village lay silent, but the wind was blowing stronger still. And the dogs were still prowling, whining and yipping, with one or two darting out from the pack, then sidling back on tiptoe.

That wind! Harder than ever, whipping the trees and picking up dust in little devil-dances. Weird weather. It felt like rain, but they said that happened only occasionally.

The dogs had gone! Perhaps they knew something the weather experts didn't...

No harm in shutting the door for a bit. He went to do it and found the wind was now a gale. And hot! Like the breath of a furnace.

Maybe one of those tropical storms was coming . He wasn't worried of course, but it'd be good to watch it from the first floor balcony. Quite dramatic in fact! He chuckled. Here he was, safe and dry and Emma would be on top of the hill by now, with all the natives and their screaming kids. They were in for a right soaking! Another tale for the lads back home.

Meanwhile, it was obvious that no rain was coming. The sky was so blue it hurt your eyes.

Then the wind stopped. Totally. Just like that! Silence... All a bit ominous. He shivered convulsively. Ugh! Someone must have walked over his grave...

Strange too, he'd seen no lightning, but wasn't that thunder? The balcony quivered. An earthquake? No! They didn't have those out here!

The balcony trembled again. The thunder (or whatever it was)

was constant now, more like a roaring.

Nervously, he glanced towards the sea.... and froze, mouth open. A cloud had appeared. Massive it was, like a long fat roll of grey cotton wool, seemingly floating just above the sea.

Heavy, smooth, fatter, taller and taller still. Calm and inexorable it came, ocean-spawned, a towering monster.

Leaning back, George had just realised that he could not see its top, when his world went away...

...and the *tsunami* rolled on.

Through the Eyes of a Baby

Anne Winnard

Alex approached the sixty-four steep steps. He sighed loudly at the daunting prospect of the twice daily enduring ascent. He was in pain, uncertain which pain was greater, the physical agony or the mental torture, misery and desperation.

Alex not only dreaded the steps in reality. Steps of many weird, terrifying descriptions would appear in his very troubled sleep, giving rise to horrendous nightmares.

The two young boys, heads down, shoulders hunched, looked almost as woebegone as their father. They held on to either side of the baby's pram.

"Stop dragging back Tom." Alex snarled at the six year old. "We're already late again."

As he spoke, Alex knew it wasn't Tom that delayed them. Tom knew this too. Tom bit his lip, scrunched up his eyes in a futile effort to hold back tears that had spilled so freely since Mum died. There never seemed to be any words of kindness or love, just a barrage of moans and complaints.

The day promised to be muggy, damp and humid; a combination that worsened Alex's condition, his limp much more pronounced; the cobbled steps even more hazardous and slippery in the humidity.

The boys and their father had devised a method for moving the pram uphill. Between them they hauled the pram up rather than pushed it, but on a day similar to this Alex had slipped and the pram rolled perilously downhill, halted by the quick thinking and agility of a young female jogger. The baby girl was unhurt but the episode led to the return of the arduous task of pushing the pram forwards.

They reached the top of the steps. The silence indicated that school had already begun.

Alex let the boys run to the playground; eight-year-old Dan

dragged his younger brother by the hand. The boys went into school by different gates. Dan was a junior school pupil and Tom still in the infant school.

Alex hobbled off as he always did in the opposite direction. He didn't look back to smile or wave. The two boys missed Mum even more. She used to take them right up to the gates, kissed and hugged each one of them as they joined their playmates. Dan said that the other boys would laugh at him, so Mum began to give Dan a kiss and hug at the top of the steps. How Dan wished Mum was here now. She could kiss and hug him as often as she chose. He closed his eyes and thought again about his plan.

Alex went to the cemetery daily. He sat by Lauren's grave and considered their family life. Lauren's life had been tragically cut short due to complications following the birth of their baby daughter. The girl had a name that Alex didn't apply. He referred to her as 'she', or just 'the girl'. Alex cared for her physical needs. He kept her clean and fed. She rarely cried, already realising her wailing would achieve nothing.

"Oh Lauren," he said. "Why did life have to be so hard? We had it all; a beautiful home, a family to be proud of. Life could not have been better. Then you left us all alone, unable to cope. It was because of you that we coped so well following my accident."

Alex and Lauren had worked hard to get away from the rough council estate. At last, with some help from both sets of parents they had managed to get a deposit together for their own house.

Alex worked a distance away from their home, but the pay was good. He travelled to work on his motorbike. One wintry, icy cold night following a long shift he lost control of the bike on black ice. Recuperation was a lengthy process, leaving him with an injury to his legs causing the right leg to be two inches shorter than the left. The injury made it impossible for Alex to return to his employment.

Between Alex and Lauren, with austere budgeting, they just about managed financially. Lauren's pregnancy was a surprise, but also a delight when a scan showed that baby number three was a girl.

"You held our baby girl in your arms for a while Lauren and then you left us so quickly," Alex sighed. "We will love you and cherish you forever."

Alex stood up ready to leave. The day suddenly felt brighter. The burden he had carried so long became lighter. He bent over to check on his baby girl. Her face shone as a smile crept across her beautiful face - Lauren's face reflected in her deep blue eyes.

"My darling girl, my beautiful Olivia! I have neglected you for too long, but no more. We will go to get your big brothers from school and then a celebration meal at McDonald's. Later we will go to see your grandparents. It's time to show you off."

Today the hill did not seem as steep. Alex believed he could run up the slope.

Alex stopped dead in his tracks. His sons were surrounded by a small group.

"Mr Jackson?" asked a small mousy looking woman. Alex nodded.

"That's me." He replied. "But why the welcoming committee?" Alex looked perplexed and bemused.

"I am Elizabeth White. I am a social worker. Social services are concerned about the safety of your children. I am here to investigate their care and well-being. I suggest we all go inside to discuss the future of your children"

"Daddy," Dan cried holding on to his teacher's hand. "I didn't mean to run away. I was looking for Nana Jenny and Grandad Pat. I got lost and a lady took me to a policeman."

"Oh Danny, I am so sorry," Alex said, dropping to his knees. "I realised today how much I have neglected you all!" Alex sobbed against his son's chest. He looked up into the eyes of Jenny, his mother in law.

"We know you suffered a tragic loss, Alex", Jenny said. "We all did. We lost our only daughter and subsequently our grandchildren. They are lonely, sad and bereft.

"You isolated yourself Alex. You refused help from your

parents, us and all your friends."

"I know," Alex said. "I have been so locked in by my own grief and misery, I gave no one else any consideration. Things will change, you'll see. I want to be there for my children, but they need more. I will accept help."

"That's good so far," said Elizabeth White, "But for the foreseeable future, we must be in regular contact. The children are our joint and main priority. Take your boys and I will be in touch."

Alex gathered the children close to him, hugging them, crying and laughing simultaneously.

Jenny cuddled Olivia the granddaughter she hardly knew. There was so much time to make up for.

"Where to boys?" Alex asked.

"Can we go to Nana's first and then to McDonald's for tea?" said Tom.

"A splendid idea, "Alex agreed. The happy group set off. Nana pushing Olivia, Dan and Tom glued fast either side of Alex.

This day heralded a new beginning for them all. They would look forward to the future with optimism and remember the past with love.

ABDUCTION

Lillian Hassall

It's hard to imagine life without him, but that's what I have to do now. He's gone forever - taken one cold November night.

I had gone to the convenience store across the road from my house. Just for a few things, milk, and bread - so insignificant now. I can't even remember all the unimportant details.

It was the phone call, a man laughing and Monty barking in the background. The man said that he would kill Monty if I didn't give him £250. Who was this? Did he know me?

Did I know him? Was he watching my every move? He said that I had to leave the money in a brown jiffy bag in the telephone box over the road and he would leave Monty inside the phone box.

Why? Oh, why did I leave Monty outside the store? I could have left him at home but I went out. My intention was to take him on his nightly walk. Twice a day, early morning and late evening, Monty looked forward to that. I only had to head for the coat hanger and he was behind me, wagging his little tail.

I have never stopped crying, asking that same question. Monty was my best friend.

I remember how I had nursed him after he had swallowed one of my muscle relaxants. He was so small and lively. Anything that fell to the floor Monty made sure he was the first there to pick it up. I remember phoning the vet. He had closed for the night, but had left an emergency number to contact. I rang the number so fast, I wasn't sure if I had missed a digit.

I was relieved when a voice said, "Emergency vet, can I help you?"

My voice was shaking, I explained what had happened.

He said, "If Monty has swallowed it we have to wait. Phone me first thing. I'm here from 8 am."

The night was so very long, Monty was screaming, shaking and falling from side to side. I boiled the kettle, filled my water bottle, lay down on the couch with the warm bottle on my stomach and held Monty close to, stroking him, talking to him, kissing him. He whimpered all night long. Eventually we both fell asleep. When the light came streaming through the window, I fully expected him to have died, but he just looked up at me with his little deadpan eyes. He wriggled to get down, wobbling went across to his bowl and had a long, long drink. Monty had come through. From that day he never went to pick anything else up off the floor.

I phoned the vet and told him that Monty had come through, I explained the events of the preceding night and that Monty knew I was there to help him.

I believe that's when we bonded, Monty and me.

When he had a bath, the whole house did. He'd skedaddle down the stairs and slip and slide across the wooden floor.

Out of nowhere a whistle blew, it kept blowing, it was the kettle. The sudden noise brought me back to the brink. Now I was crying again. Where are you Monty?

That night, I had left £250 in a brown jiffy bag on the shelf in the phone box, just like the man asked me to. I didn't even call the police. I should have, but I didn't. I ran back to my house so fast. Maybe just in time to peep from behind my curtain to see my beloved Monty sitting in the phone box. But nothing. I waited and waited - but nothing. I wanted him back so badly. I couldn't think straight. I found it hard to do my work. My house was in disarray. My life had come to a standstill. I thought of parents whose children had been abducted and prayed that they be reunited soon.

Who was this that had entered my life? Why? There was no answer.

Then one morning I awoke. The sun was shining through my window. There was no more fretting, I had prayed every single night and day for the strength to get through this. From somewhere light was entering not only my eyes, but my ears, my mind. I wanted Monty back so now must do something. I stretched. I showered, got dressed and searched for my photo album. I knew it wasn't far away because I had been looking at so many photographs of Monty. I came across one, went across to my printer and ran off at least 50 copies. I just kept on copying till the ink ran dry.

Now, out I went pinning them up on every lamp post, tree, shop front and in the library. Now, back home to wait. Thoughts came back about that night, I went back to the phone box and I searched for the brown jiffy bag, but it was nowhere to be found. He must have watched me run back to the house and retrieved the bag and the money. But no Monty. Days had gone by - nothing.

Then one day in early March a knock came to my front door, I had just come from work. I could hear whimpering, was I hearing things. When I opened the door, a lady stood there. To be honest, I didn't take a lot of notice. Before I knew what I was doing, I was sat on the welcome foot-mat with Monty scampering, jumping all over me, licking me. Oh, I couldn't believe it.

"Where have you been? I've been looking for you everywhere."

We sat there cuddling each other, there was no mention of time, it was blissful. Suddenly the lady came into view.

"Oh!" I said, "I'm so sorry, do come in. Where did you find him?"

She told me the story of one November night, it had been raining. Her phone stopped working, so she went to the local telephone box, there was no light, as she opened the door she heard a small whimper.

"… it was this beautiful little dog, no name, no collar, no lead. I had no idea whose it was. I picked him up and put him under my coat to keep him warm and dry and brought him home. I went to my mother's for Christmas and New Year and decided to bring him with me. It wasn't until the other day, I saw the photographs all over the place, I'm really sorry you must have gone through so much."

After telling her my story about Monty being abducted, I said, "It was then you must have found him. It was just split second timing!"

I have found my best friend and made another.

A Fading Beauty

Lillian Hassall

In the corner of a quiet room

A flower, beautiful in all its bloom

A sweet scented rose with deep red petals

Soft and velvet its glandular cells

Its stance is small yet oh so grand.

Its delicate face held in my hand

A month or more it gives me pleasure

To see and smell God's given treasure.

Love I bestow on this exquisite flower

Constant care and attention hour by hour

A fading beauty, in its last display

To rise and bloom another day.

Rex – The Philosopher King

Alan Rick

I suppose most children must see their relatives as inhabitants of a benign world of eccentricity. Mine, headed by my grandmother, were no exception. But my Aunty Gladys, a lady of surreal thinking, managed to dispense with rational thought altogether and plunge into a mental world which none of us was ever able to penetrate.

She was that specialist home-grown product of English soil – the doting animal lover. Her own pride and joy was Rex – a shambling pile of canine fur with no particular looks to speak of and no discernible purpose in life other than to amble through each day as it came. But to Aunty Gladys, though to no-one else, there was far more to Rex than this. We would often be treated to examples of his vast intellect.

"Be careful what you talk about," we were cautioned "He understands every word you say." We looked at Rex for evidence of this but this always escaped us since all Rex ever did was to fix the opposite wall with a baleful stare.

"He's thoughtful," Aunty Gladys would add as we expressed doubt concerning his famed powers of reasoning. "He's considering things."

Much as we tried to picture Rex as the Philosopher King or as some sort of canine Confucius, the attempt was always dashed by the fact that all he ever did was to stare morosely at the opposite wall. He could hardly have derived inspiration from the wall which was covered with dull, brown wallpaper with no pattern on it.

"He's having an idea." Our aunt would insist. Apparently whenever Rex stared, this meant that he was having an idea. Following this bizarre logic, his head must have been as a full as a fully populated beehive, as staring was all he ever did.

The truth was that Rex had only two ideas – to eat when food was placed in front of him, to accompany the staring, and to sleep when it was not!

All criticism of Rex was spurned by his deluded owner on the grounds that he was "Subject to deep emotional feelings". "He's sensitive you know, he gets upset if people say unkind things about him." Again we would look at Rex for signs of emotional turbulence, for outbursts against injustices spoken against him but he just stared at the wall. Rex was as emotional as a wax figure – compared to Rex the goldfish was beside itself. The fish would gently waft its tail in an elegant and quite expressive gesture. Rex stared. There was no poetry in Rex.

In time Rex became slower in his movements, if that were possible, until even staring at the wall seemed to demand more effort than he was able to summon. He ended his days before a roaring open fire. It was then that our aunt felt able to disclose to us what, it seemed, had often passed between them in our absence.

"He sometimes had some sorry words to say about you two boys when you used to scoff at his lively mind." So Rex could talk as well!

It's often said, quite rightly that our pet animals should be well looked after, but perhaps there are cases where the owner should be taken into care as well.

ONE MINUTE

Mavis Crowe

One minute I am young,

Next minute I am old.

One minute I am a bride,

Next minute I am a grieving widow.

One minute I am a mother, given my first born to hold,

Next minute I have my first grandson.

One minute I have lots of friends,

Next minute they are gone.

One minute I have a job,

Next minute that's gone too.

One minute my home is full of people,

Next minute I sit alone.

Would I have changed anything in my life?

NO!

Not for one minute

OH BETH WHERE IS THY STING?

Bill Cameron

Some may look forward to dawn to dusk sunshine, wall to wall clear blue skies and the air heavy with pollen and saturated with the fragrance of flowers. But not me, Elizabeth the worker bee.

I hate these long days and today, Midsummer Day, more than any other. We're expected to be out of the hive as soon as the sun rises and work through the whole day flitting from flower to flower to hive and back again until the sun goes down.

That's the price of being one of the workers, like us girls, who have to do everything. The younger ones stay at home doing the cleaning, nursing, building the comb and taking charge of the 'catering' with nectar and honey. The more mature ladies, like me, are sent out harvesting pollen and nectar or defending the hive from intruders. Paul's letter to the Corinthians mentions the ferocity of a similarly named antecedent of mine in 'Oh Beth where is thy sting?'

Do you know what? If we had a life span longer than a few months, we would be unionised and campaigning the Queen for compliance with the European Working Time Directive – but all you get from the workforce is 'Life's too short for confrontational politics'.

By the way, we admire and adore our own Queen. Our envy is moderated when someone reminds us that she will lay up to a thousand eggs every day – it brings tears to my eyes just to think about it.

As for the men. If the drones could only get their testosterone under control we might get some support, but, all they do is hang around the hive living on nectar and honey – each one boasting about the size of his proboscis. You can see the origin of the human expression 'Lazy Bee'. Once they're tanked up enough they're off out, looking for a queen to impregnate and propagate a new colony. It's just as well the males will then immediately expire. They leave the hive full of bravado and machismo, then wham! Bam! thank you ma'am! and he's another dead drone.

Looking back, I think my younger days were better even if the work was hard. These days, my job isn't finished when I get back and pass on my cargo to the youngsters. I have to do this frenzied dervish dance to direct my sister field bees to my floral source. My friend Hilda is sadly getting past it. Not only is her memory going in her dotage but her sciatica prevents her moving as accurately as she used to. She has frequently sent harvesters miles off course. Some never came back. Do you ever wonder why some bees hover round dust bins?

Whilst I'm on the subject of mental alacrity and the lack of it, it is claimed that we bees share a common ancestry with those dumb thugs the wasps. I don't think so. Bees are far superior mentally to those snarling yobs, who always want an opportunity to flash their stingers. Not an ounce of sense in the whole species. It's quite obvious when you see ten times more stupid wasps smeared over windows than you see intelligent bees.

And don't ask me about hornets. You don't need me to tell you about the BNP of the insect world and what a moronic bunch of dung dwellers they are.

I can usually avoid head on conflict with these pariahs when I'm out and about by keeping away from picnics, so it's mostly enjoyable getting out of the house. Peace and quiet and the smell of fresh air are better than the environment of smelly squealing larvae. Some gardens nowadays have a magnificent display of colour and plethora of aromas which delight the senses of my flypast.

History tells of a time of unbroken miles of hedgerow and meadow with an equal abundance and wider variety of interesting birds to avoid. Sparrows and Starlings are not serious predators to a bee with two compound and three simple eyes in her head.

Of course, it's only work – work – work until the rain comes. When we're grounded in the hive it can get a bit claustrophobic and the young workers have their work cut out keeping us cool and ventilated with their wings fanning the air around the hive.

So next time you're tempted to waft away a buzzing insect from your food, please look carefully and listen to our plea:

If it's a bee, leave it be,

If it's a wasp tell it "get lost!"

AT FOX GILL HOUSE

Shaun Kelly

The four-by-four pickup sways along the cinder track and Tony finally sees his cottage coming fully into view. He stops, opens the gate, drives through into the tiny courtyard, gets out and does not bother to close the gate against the sheep on the hillside. His thought is entirely on a mug of coffee, provided the propane is OK and on doing things before nightfall, as the Jenny has been temperamental lately.

As usual for Fox Gill House, when he is alone here he starts talking to himself. Perhaps this takes the edge off the silence for him.

"Tony baby, you are not a happy bunny. Why have you just downed tools on the Harrison job and driven seventy miles up to Fox Gill House here? Beats me, baby."

The cottage, his cottage in the sticks, is barely one third rebuilt as it should be. Winter is coming on. The slow crawl of electricity over the fields and moors to the Orange phone mast has stalled because of geology (of all things) and the spring giving him water has begun to clog again. Plus - and this is their biggest disaster of the lot - Fiona told him today she is packing in working for him.

She had said, leaning around Harrison's new soil stack, "Boss, I can't find another way to say this so I'm gonna tell you quickly like, but I'm handing in my cards on Saturday."

Tony plugs on with making the coffee.

He says aloud to the untiled kitchen wall;

"Fiona, where in God's name am I going to find someone with your level of skill? Handing in your cards? What ARE cards anyway because it's all done on line now, Fiona? And just because your bloody biological clock got ticking and I can see myself you're five months up the duff. What sort of a reason is that?"

But even Tony knew it was a very good reason indeed.

Fiona with a distinct lump, looking green around the gills in the mornings, avoiding the ladder, being all-too-careful when lifting stuff;

"Why didn't you tell me, Fiona? Instead of which you cut me off at the knees. Really, you might have told me. I'm not just your employer you know."

It is true too. Fiona is unusual in the building game. She is a pretty woman in her early to middle twenties working with a guy of fifty-odd and in all weathers. Of course, as Tony guesses, the other tradesmen make the usual remarks and obscene gestures behind Tony's back, but never to his face, probably because Tony is a big fit guy and an ex-boxer who still trains twice a week regularly.

The guys are good with Fiona though. They josh her and sometimes some guy in the pub makes an off-colour joke but Tony reckons they are proud of her too.

When Fiona started working for him Tony's Rule Number One with her was *'No Funny Business. Play It Absolutely Straight with Her'* and there had been no funny business and other people could think what they liked.

He sits down on the rickety seat by the iron table outside the side door, sips his mug of coffee. He looks out over the piles of unused gravel and sand dumped too close to the doorway and addresses the hillside outside like a Shakespearian.

"Yvonne, how come it never worked out with us? I was happy. You were happy - sometimes. All right, I was away a deal on refurbs in the Midlands and you got fed up with me because I was never there for you. But I did my best, Yvonne. I looked after Fiona like you asked me to. I did my best."

Fiona is the daughter of Tony's ex-partner Yvonne but when Tony and Yvonne split up Fiona still wanted to carry on working with Tony. To learn the business, she says. Now, she is almost on a par in skill with Tony himself.

A kind of resigned sarcastic humour sweeps over him.

"You might really have been my daughter, Fee. Not just my worker, my workmate. If Yvonne and me had stuck at it I guess we would have got hitched in the end and you would be my real daughter now, Fiona. Me becoming a grandfather."

A resilient kind of guy, Tony is not the self-pitiful type to cry into his beer but the words *'daughter'* and *'grandfather'* suddenly hurt him like hell.

He shouts out, "You could have lived up here, Fee, at Fox Gill House. Had a family up here with this guy I never clapped eyes on, had a good life. Me and your mother coming up weekends maybe. Calling me *Tony* and not *Boss*. Yeah Tony. When did you ever once call me Tony? Never. How do you think that makes me feel?

"OK, OK Fiona. No more working side by side or hauling worktops and roof laths and fence posts. No more sitting in the van when it's too wet to work and eating sandwiches and reading the papers side by side."

He is shouting again, shouting against the silence.

He takes a leak beyond the gooseberry bushes in the garden - thinks about going back to the Harrison job tomorrow. Going back after a cold night below unaired sheets and, probably, his old army greatcoat. Just peachy.

He also thinks about Fiona leaving him on Saturday.

"I don't think a double Jammie's and a pint of lager is quite right, Tony baby, do you? Not for Fee anyhow. A Thank You gift I guess, plus a card. Thank You for all your hard work, Fiona, and may all your troubles be little ones. Corny, but it's what folk put on Thank You cards when someone is up the duff. Buy her an enormous bunch of flowers too, expensive ones."

He wipes his eyes and prepares himself to do battle with the generator.

Aloud he says to the two sheep at the gate. "Do I sign the cards *'Tony'* or *'Boss'*? Or *Your pal Tony* or *Your Boss Toy'*? Or *Affectionately Your boss Tony* or *It's been great, Tony*?"

What Tony the employer will NOT write on the cards - and Tony knows this perfectly well - is *With All My Love, Fiona, I will miss you desperately, Tony* and with four kisses attached.

He makes for the shed to grab an armful of cedar logs to light the iron stove in the dining room. And he knows he will miss her too, desperately.

SEASONS

Lillian Hassall

And the seasons are changing
The months are rearranging
There's a mountain of snow where the path should be
The only way across is up and over, It's hard to see
The fog descends, the bitter haze nibbles at your face
The frozen dew falls like tiny crystals out of space
And the seasons are changing
The months are rearranging
The vast array of colour pushes its way through the earth
Trees stand stately, heavily laden with new birth
A multitude of birds warble their dawn chorus
Hedgehogs, squirrels, small rodents that hibernate in our forest.
And the seasons are changing
The months are rearranging
Sunshine fills the early morning sky
Woodland pools are aglow where the playful
children laugh and play all day long
Green fields abundant with flowers beyond
And the seasons are changing
The months are rearranging
The shadows are lower, the trees are shedding their leaves
Bronze, golden, evergreen, it is hard to believe
yet another year has gone by, how and why?
Seasons fill our lives with an amazing journey as time goes by.
And the seasons are changing
The months are rearranging.

The Pied Piper of Hamelin – The Rat's Story

Mavis Crowe

I gradually opened my eyes. How long had I been asleep, I did not know. I felt weak and hungry. Trying to get my thoughts together, I began to remember the last piece of meat I had eaten. I knew as I tasted it something was wrong. The pains started and the last thing I remember was curling up in a small ball at the back of our overcrowded nest.

Unsteadily I got to my feet. The nest was quiet and eerie. Where were all my family? There was usually at least fifty or sixty of us packed into the small hole. Now it was empty.

We had all lived comfortably here in the Squire's mansion. There was always plenty to eat. The Squire was a wealthy man and lots of food would be wasted but we would always finish it off.

Creeping out of my home in the kitchen I could see the ankles of the fat old cook. She would normally be shouting and screaming - often with a large stick in her hand waving it about and trying to hit one of us. Some days many of us would run round her legs, nibbling at her already well-bitten ankles until she would just sit down and cry. What fun we could have with her.

However today she was calm and even humming a pleasant tune as she prepared the Squire's dinner.

Feeling too weak and hungry to play games I hurried past as quietly as I could. The best place to go would be the market. Even though it was late and most of the discarded products would have already gone, consumed by the thousands of rats who would assemble there. I may however find a few scraps - enough to keep me going for tonight.

Arriving, I couldn't believe my eyes there was fruit, meat, vegetables and bread. But no other rats.

What had happened? Now I began to feel frightened and very lonely.

Just then I heard a small squeak and there, hiding behind a crate, was the most beautiful creature I had ever seen. Her coat was brown and shiny. Her white teeth protruded from her small delicate mouth.

"Wow how glad I am to see you. I thought I was the only one left."

"OH!" she cried, "so did I."

"What has happened? Where has every one gone?"

She began to tell the story of how a human had come wearing bright coloured clothes, playing a pipe.

"The tune was haunting;" she said, "Rats came from everywhere and started to follow him. I tried to keep up but my front leg had been caught in a trap and I was unable to walk. That was two days ago - and none of them have returned."

I put my tail over her back.

"Come with me," I said, "I will look after you."

Back at the mansion she couldn't believe her eyes.

"Oh what a beautiful place you live in. I lived by the river in the sewage outlet"

We lived quietly not wanting to cause trouble. We stayed out of the way of the cook but carried on eating the food which she always left lying about.

It wasn't too long before I became a father and then a grandfather and even a great grandfather. Our nest was once again getting full. Some of the younger ones left to make homes of their own.

The only advice I could give them was to stay out trouble and not to annoy humans. Most importantly of all was never, ever; follow a stranger wearing bright coloured clothes playing a pipe.

CHRISTMAS BOUNTY

Lillian Hassall

The latest games the latest toys,

Santa came to visit every year.

He dropped his booty down the chimney -

For all the good girls and boys.

Once Christmas Day was out of the way

Good kids would play with the cardboard.

Mum and Dad would scrimp and scrape

And pay all year for Santa's hoard.

Oh deary me how can it be?

"The children were bored," we hear parents say.

They have so much, how can this be?

Maybe we should sack Santa and just enjoy Christmas Day!

1066

Alan Rick

The scene is Hastings, Sussex, immigration office - the year 1066.

A Saxon civil servant tears up a scroll of parchment bearing the name *Erik the Viking*, throws it in the waste bin, puts down his quill pen and shouts "Next!"

The door opens and yet another asylum seeker walks in. The immigration officer says at first without looking up, "Good morning, I believe you want to seek asylum?"

The immigrant replies, "That is correct."

"Name please."

"Duke"

"I beg your pardon," says the officer – while he's thinking "Duke? What sort of bloody name is that? Why can't these people give their children proper names these days?"

"Oh, Sorry, Duke William, that is."

"I see. And where have you travelled from?"

"Normandy"

The officer writes down the information, "Duke William of Normandy" on the parchment.

"All right. May I see your passport, please?"

William draws his sword. "I usually find that this guarantees me entry and safe passage without let or hindrance, through any country I choose to visit."

"Yes, well that seems to be in order. May I ask what the main purpose of your stay in England is?"

"Conquest as it happens. Well mainly conquest with a bit of pillaging and looting thrown in, I suppose."

The official frowns a little, "Hmm, Yes. But what do you see as the legal basis for your claim to asylum?"

"Oh, it's quite straightforward really. My army is bigger than your army."

"Well I'm afraid I'll have to ask you to fill in these forms. There are rather a lot of them, but…"

William interrupts, "What? Oh no! We Norman barons don't do *creative writing*. As a matter of fact, none of us can read or write. We leave that pansy nonsense to the clergy. They're always going around mumbling to themselves and reading books and stuff. No. We do war – that's what we do."

"I have to ask you – do you intend to engage in gainful employment while you are in this country as I must point out that this could affect your entitlement to benefits."

"We certainly intend to claim benefits, but we're quite happy to leave the gainful employment part to your lot. Your peasants can work the fields and produce the food. Our job is to consume it. It's a partnership really."

"Aha. Since you do not actually work as such are you saying

you would like to draw benefits straight away?"

"Absolutely. To begin with, we'll have Kent, Surrey, Middlesex, Wessex and Norfolk. We'll collect the rest when we've settled in a bit."

"I understand that you propose to offer the Saxons an insurance policy."

"That's right, we call it the *feudal system*. It's a policy with generous protection from horrible visitors, Swedes, Goths, Visigoths, Vikings and such like. And it only costs them eighty five percent of their produce."

"What if some of the Saxons decide not to take out your policy?"

"Well, then our *double indemnity* guarantee comes into effect. Whilst we can't guarantee one hundred percent that their home won't be burned down if they have the policy – we can guarantee that it will be if they don't. The policy is fully comprehensive."

"All right then. Have you any dependents?"

"Yes. Two hundred barons fully armed and ready to draw benefits right away. We're not related but I regard them all as my stepsons."

"Stepsons? Why stepsons?"

"Because, my little quill pushing Saxon, if any of your staff turn awkward, they step on you. We Normans are not without a sense of humour, you know."

The officer signs the form, stamps it and says, "We've taken into consideration all the arguments of the case. I think I may say that your application for asylum and full benefits will be granted."

"Much obliged and may I say at once that we have both shown today that a negotiated settlement in a friendly manner is always better than vulgar brute force."

My Frank

Barry Seddon

We had been together for nearly fifty years when my Frank started to change. For all the time I'd known him, he had been like his name - open, honest, trusting and fair. A man who knew what was right and acted accordingly.

At the railway yards he had been the same, "one of the lads," an organiser who never bullied. And he always told me, always consulted me. We were a team, I suppose. A team full of love and affection, where a kiss was never far away.

The change began so quickly. It was Hallowe'en. We'd had tea and were sitting quietly when the doorbell chimed. I smiled, expecting Frank's usual joke...."Avon calling!" Silence.

I'll never forget that moment. I had just glanced up, and seen Frank staring ahead, deadpan. The bell chimed again, children giggled and in an instant, my lovely man became a stranger

"Frank! Are you alright?"

He twitched as I spoke and when he turned to look at me, I almost shouted in shock. There was nothing behind his eyes. Then he frowned and the frown became something more like a snarl, eyes narrowed, brows down, lips curled.

I think I must have gasped. Then he shouted "NO!" loud and frightened, his eyes rolled up, then closed and he began to shiver. I was on my feet and had taken one step towards him, when he went still and seemed to fall asleep.

After that, everything happened in a soft-edged haze.....999, soothing ambulance men, A and E, into a ward for overnight observation, kind nurses, cups of tea, slice of toast, no sleep.

"Idiopathic convulsion," said the doctor.

"Means they don't know what caused it," said the nurse.

They were right though, when they said it was unlikely to

happen again. Back home, I was on edge for days but there were no more fits. Frank seemed to be making a slow recovery from whatever it was and I began to relax. I suppose I became a bit complacent because I was taken completely by surprise when fate stepped in again and dealt me the next bad card.

This time it was far worse, because it was a long and slow process, during which I had to watch, helpless, as little by little, my Frank became someone else.

It began with little things, the sort we've all done. He'd start a sentence, stop halfway through, start again several times, then shake his head, and shrug his shoulders, saying "No good. It's gone." And smiling, a heart-breaking glimpse of his happier self, he'd say: "Never mind! Must have been a lie."

Lately though it has got worse. More and more often I've found him standing somewhere in the house, looking bewildered and lost. One awful day I found him in the garden wearing trousers, a white shirt and carpet slippers, standing there, just standing and staring, with the rain coming down like stair-rods. And wherever I found him, he was never able to explain why he was there.

His railway bosses in the engine shed were wonderful. "He's getting on a bit. He's just day-dreaming." Then, inevitably, "It would be for the best if you could persuade him to retire, Mrs Jacobs. He'll get a good pension."

But my Frank, my lost and lovely Frank, would turn his head away in silence if I tried to say anything. It felt cruel to keep on at him.

It progressed. Quite often he would come home late because he'd forgotten where to get off the bus. Several neighbours told me he had walked past them without even saying hello. "As though he'd never known me," said one.

He would return from a little errand to the corner shop. He knew how to get there because he could see our gatepost from the shop door. But he'd return with the wrong things.

Sometimes he would set off for work on a Sunday; other times he would forget to shave; or he would pick up a drink and spill it if he didn't hold it with both hands. At first things were happening just now and again, but then it was more often -- he became less and less able to use a knife and fork for instance. Then I had to buy new shoes with Velcro fasteners when tying shoe-laces became impossible. Cardigans with zips were out too, but I still had to fasten the buttons on the new ones.

Then at last his bosses had no choice but to pension him off and that's when the withdrawal set in.

I was driven close to despair, sleepless and afraid of what might happen if I let Frank out of my sight. Then one night, just a year on from that Hallowe'en, I answered the door to find the doctor there. A neighbour had called him, worried after seeing Frank standing at the front window, staring out "like somebody not right".

The doctor and I were talking when there was a crash and the sound of breaking glass. We found Frank standing in the living room amid fragments of mirror.

"Stranger at the window!" he shouted. "Stranger! I hit him!"

It was his own reflection...

The doctor explained, as kindly as he could, that Frank was nearing the point where I could no longer cope. Frank's dementia was the kind called Alzheimer's, when loss of physical control would often lead to frustrated anger and sometimes to violence, as happened with the mirror.

"I'm sorry Mrs Jacobs, but I'm afraid the next step will have to be into care," said the doctor. "Frank always gave you his love. Now you can relax a bit and give it back."

So now my Frank is being properly looked after. I see him a lot and he seems quite happy. From what I've read, there are all sorts of better treatments coming along. People also seem to be more sympathetic. Perhaps it's because they know more about it. It's no longer a mysterious thing to be whispered about.

As I said earlier, when this all started we'd been together for nearly fifty years   Next year is the golden one.

FRIENDSHIP

Guest writer Eric MacKinder

*Friendship is the comfort -
the inexpressible comfort,
of feeling safe with someone.
Having neither to measure nor weigh thoughts
just as they are.
The chaff and the grain together.
Certain that a kind and friendly hand
will take and sift them.
Keep what is worth keeping
and with a breath of comfort
blow the rest away.*

BILLY JOE AND I

Anne Winnard

Billy Joe and I had been best pals for most of our lives. We had grown up like brothers in Tallahatchie. He was always there for me. I could confide in him and I knew he would respect my confidentiality.

He was a cautious sort, reserved, handsome and physically very active. He taught me how to climb a tree, how to skin a rabbit; to dive from the bridge and land confidently in the water.

When I heard of his death I knew instinctively he had not jumped. That was completely out of character. If he had jumped he would not have made any mistakes. Someone else was responsible for his death. Indirectly I felt responsible. I was with him early morning that day. I certainly wasn't the last person to see him alive.

Billy Joe was so organised and kept check regularly on his appearance and financial status.

He was committed in all types of relationships, friends and family. Many girls tried to lure him into an intimate relationship, but Billy Joe was not prepared for that. He confided in me that when it did happen it would be for the rest of his life.

When I first asked Billy Joe to help me sort out my latest problem, he replied with a shrug of his shoulders and said, "Are you serious?" I knew he would eventually agree. He was always cautious and would think long and hard before making a decision.

He met me soon after sunrise that fateful day. As always he was smartly dressed, clean shaven, hair groomed smartly in place. He was going for an interview for a place in college later that day. Billy Joe was one for keeping up appearances. I envied him the way he could attract people. He was charismatic; a man of few words, whereas I was eloquent, I could attract an audience, but was unable to follow my words with action. Sex was always on my mind and that is exactly where it stayed!

I would approach a girl eagerly anticipating the action that would follow my conversation. I would visualise myself in some of the positions in the Kamasutra book. I could recite whole passages from memory.

Part way through my introductory speech, I became stifled and struggled, stammered and stuttered.

About to ask a girl out, I would stammer, "......d d do y y y you th th think?"

No wonder I had many disastrous and changeable partners.

Billy Joe used to say that I was naive and needed to grow up. I was so gullible. That is what had carried me into the awful mess I found myself in and ultimately led to Billy Joe's demise.

Mary Jane approached me and asked me to help her cousin with some work he needed to do. She made up to me, made me feel good, alive and wanted. Naively I agreed because she promised to be my date for the next village dance. Wow, she was so pretty. I would have agreed to do anything.

I was to meet Mary Jane, her cousin and some of his gang in the soda bar two towns east of my town. I was unfamiliar with the place. No one recognised me. The plan was that I should approach storekeepers of small towns. I would be notified when I would be required five hours before.

"You're so good with words," Mary Jane whispered in my ear. "You can sweet talk anyone and get them to do what you want."

Flattery in my case gets you anywhere. I was totally mesmerised. She had me under her spell.

My job was to approach small businesses, chat to them, gain their confidence; meanwhile my colleagues would remove anything of value. Mary Jane would come along later to collect me. I was never accused by anyone. I was so proud of myself and my love for Mary Jane deepened.

On completion of my penultimate job I was presented with a heavy metal safe. I kept it hidden in the cotton shed until the code could be broken. I called round to Mary Jane's uninvited and unexpectedly. I wanted to surprise her, but the surprise was mine.

Mary Jane already had a guest, a very intimate guest. I left. I realised I had been duped. I was heartbroken. I made my way to Billy Joe, told him the whole lot and begged for his help to get rid of the safe.

We met at sunrise, heaved the safe onto his pickup truck and headed for the Tallahatchie Bridge. Together we hoisted the metal box into the river.

Someone had followed. We went our separate ways. At lunchtime I heard the awful news, Billy Joe was dead.

Two days later I was arrested for my part in the robberies. No one else was involved. I kept quiet.

Papa died that year, my brother moved away and Mammy gave up and died from a broken heart.

I'm still in prison, soon to be released. What lies ahead? I have no idea!

I have made the most of my time here. I learned how to give a public speech; how to write and most importantly how to say NO.

Oh yes and there's the stash of cash to be collected. Billy Joe had cracked the code before we hoisted the safe over the bridge. I'm off East to New York.

Of course the whole account is fictional. I'm actually a criminal and spend my time in prison in an imaginary place concocting stories in my brain. Some inmates believe me, some don't, but they all love my stories and fantasies!

The Interview

Alan Rick

The scene:

The Head teacher's run-down office in an underperforming school.

The Players

Roger: Chairman of Board of Governors

Susan: Applicant for a teaching position.

ROGER: WELL NOW MISS – ER …?

Susan Muggins

Roger: Ah yes – Miss Muggins – knew it was something like that – I believe you wish to be apply for the position of teacher at this school?

Susan That is correct – I wish to broaden my horizons a little.

ROGER: YES. I THINK THEY MAY BE STRETCHED BEYOND BREAKING POINT. STILL. WHAT ARE YOUR QUALIFICATIONS?

SUSAN I HAVE A BA HONOURS IN HISTORY AND A MA IN PHILOSOPHY AND A PH. D.

ROGER: REALLY? THAT'S MOST IMPRESSIVE. IT'S MORE THAN THE ENTIRE STAFF OF THE SCHOOL HAS ADDED TOGETHER.

SUSAN HOW ARE THEY QUALIFIED?

ROGER: WELL, THERE'S MR WINKS – HE HAS A PASS IN WOODWORK AND MISS TREDBULL – SHE GOT 9 OUT OF 10 FOR ARITHMETIC IN HER PRIMARY SCHOOL. THAT'S ABOUT IT I'M AFRAID.

SUSAN WHAT ARE THE SCHOOL'S SCHOLASTIC ATTAINMENTS?

ROGER: SCHOLASTIC … EH?

SUSAN THEIR ACADEMIC LEVEL.

ROGER: Oh, you mean exam results? Not much to report on that front I'm afraid – although we did have a boy pass an 'O' level once – erm – 1976 it was – his father gave him some help.

Susan What – coached him?

ROGER: Good Lord no – we got his father to sit the exam in his place. The boy wouldn't have been able to write his name – we once wrote the letters of his name in random order - he still couldn't work it out.

Susan I hear your headmistress has rather old fashioned ideas on discipline – is that so?

ROGER: Old fashioned! She's medieval – still hasn't got used to the idea that beheading is no longer legal.

Susan I hear she has plans to extend the facilities of the school.

ROGER: Yes – but they were turned down by the authorities as being not in line with modern education practice.

Susan What did she have in mind?

ROGER: The gallows!

Susan I have had a peep into your art class – there was a young lady standing on a chair with no clothes on.

ROGER: Ah – that was the art mistress Miss Lushbot – perhaps I will introduce you when you are a little more accustomed to our ways,

Susan I was told I would be meeting the deputy headmistress as well as yourself.

ROGER: Ah that is Miss Wrench – she is unfortunately on ... erm. 'Vacation' at the moment for a period of six months.

Susan Seems a long time for a holiday.

ROGER: Well yes – but the actual length of her stay was not her choice do you see?

SUSAN Is she happy where she is?

CHAIR: I'm sure she is. The accommodation is of the – shall we say – secure type and there are others there who have her specialist skills.

SUSAN If appointed when would I start my duties?

ROGER: How about in ten minutes' time? – You are the first applicant we have had in four years.

SUSAN Very well – I accept.

ROGER: Good God! – I mean welcome Miss Muggins and may I wish you all the luck you may need.

COCKLE WOMAN

Shaun Kelly

My Aunty Dola and me sit there on a rock and watch an oil tanker slowly moving on a solid block of calm blue ocean and along the horizon from one side to the other.

Warm May sunshine and a tiny warm breeze and very few people around us at Limeslade Bay today because the kids are still at school.

My Aunty Dola hands me a clump of seaweed to sniff and I remember the edible stuff known as laverbread comes from this very stretch of coast, though this isn't it. Aunty Dola is my mother's sister and she is famous in our family for once being a cockle woman at Penclywd on the other side of The Gower.

"So you were telling me about this Colin, Angelica, who is your second cousin, lovely, and my first cousin of course, Bryn's son."

I still look out to sea. "Well, you know, aunty, you guessed didn't you, when I came here yesterday out of the blue? You guessed how it is, didn't you?"

"'Well, Angelica, I wondered what you are doing here on The Gower when you should be at college like, miles away from here. Our cousin Colin, I suppose it's him is it, is the father?'

I just can't answer. I sit here feeling I am watching the wrong play. Not me at all.

Aunty Dola says, thoughtfully, "All mouth and trousers that one. Good-looking mind, even now, though he can't be much less than forty if he's a day. Disgraceful really, with you only eighteen."

Out at sea the oil tanker sails peacefully on.

"Mind, he was much better looking once. Had his nose broken you know."

I say "That flat nose of his, yes. He told me once he played rugby for the Welsh Under-Nineteens. Scrum half. Broken in a match with a French team"

"Well, lovely, he did play rugby once, Colin. He was very fit once, our Colin. It wasn't rugby that broke his nice nose though. Something else broke Colin's nose, like."

I say, 'What was that then, aunty?'

Aunty Dola says, slyly, "My fist. That's what broke it, lovely. I broke it for him. Want to know what for?"

I say I have no idea what for.

"Trying it on. Trying it on, and I was a married woman of forty myself at the time, though I was a bit of a looker, like. Trying it on, when my husband was away on the oil rig in The States."

I say, dully I suppose, "He was always smarming and flattering my mum, but after a while he started catching me when I was on my own. I liked the attention. The first time, when he went a lot further, it was only just after my period so I was OK. The second time was in the middle of the month, so I wasn't."

Dola grips my bare arm. Her hand is strong.

"Water under the bridge, lovely."

Silence, except for seagulls and the breeze.

"Like I say, Angelica, he does the self-same nonsense with me, lovely, putting his arm round me, chatting me up. This same Colin. But I push him off, see. Then he tries again and his hands are going where they shouldn't go with a married woman, you know, so I push him off again."

I sort of recognise this pattern.

"He tries it again and I completely lose my rag don't I? I just draw back my fist and I ram it straight into the middle of his face, bang! Well, his nose explodes like I'd hit a grapefruit with a hammer. Colin, he does no more than drop down onto my carpet, like a sack of coal, with blood everywhere."

I suppose I am looking at her with opened eyes.

"Helluva mess, lovely. Well, of course despite all this nonsense

Colin is family to me and my husband isn't he? So I get quite worried and eventually I get an ambulance for him to go to the hospital at Brynmill."

Despite her supposed worry my Aunty Dola is laughing heartily, perched next to me on our rock, and despite myself I join in with her.

"Very soon, all the locals are talking about him, and me. For a fortnight after, every time I went out on our road my neighbours pretended to be frightened of me and I would raise my right arm like this and clench my fist and it was all lovely. Lovely, lovely. They called me *The Battling Cockle Woman of Penclywd*."

We laugh together, more relaxed, almost happy, despite my news. Eight weeks at least now.

"But Colin, the poor dab, everybody is laughing at him. His nose broke by a woman! He gets laughed out of town. No real man at all, Angelica."

Our oil tanker goes behind the cliffs and out of sight.

Dola puts her strong old arm around my shoulders and says slowly "It isn't the end of the world you know. Life goes on." She stops, seems to be thinking. "Your own mother got caught, Angelica. My sister Gwen. Caught like you."

I turn sharp towards her. My face must be a picture.

"She never told me, Aunty."

"She wouldn't, would she? She didn't tell your father either, and for God's sake don't breathe a word to her or your father. She'll kill me."

"What happened, Aunty?"

"Same story. Not Colin though but a man similar. All mouth and trousers. Your mother thought he was the biggest thing since sliced bread, but for me he was too smooth and plausible by a damn sight and your mother got caught."

Caught. An old phrase for the twenty-first century.

"Sixteen weeks, lovely. Course, Gwen and me are very close as you know and I go with her to the clinic for the operation. She was very ill, my poor Gwen. Terrible. And the lies we had to tell were even worse, lovely."

The next morning, I catch the coach back home and straightaway I tell my mother I'm pregnant, but I knew she knew already.

My mother does not ask who the father is and I think afterwards, with me going off to Wales to see her sister Dola, she quickly puts two and two together and makes a very enormous four. Colin is never likely to cross our doorstep again.

After my operation I grieve for the life which is lost, but in a distant, detached, lonely way. I lie in bed and I think about Mum. I wonder how all our lives might have been different if she'd had the baby and kept it. I wonder how well or how badly I might have been treated by this older brother or sister.

How well or how badly they might have protected me from other people, or from myself.

As I drift off to sleep at the clinic I hear in my head my Aunty Dola saying, "There's lovely," to me as I kiss her goodbye at the coach station in the city.

"Chin up, Angelica. Life goes on."

There's lovely.

Pleasures of Long Ago

Mary Connor

*It`s been many years and I suppose for some
It really wouldn`t have mattered.
But for me the pain of needing you
Made my whole life feel so shattered.
Soft and sweet you always were
And time has made you better.*

*But she was mum, as she would say
And my needs were all above her.
She took away my only vice
My one and only pleasure.
So I promised God if he helped, I would refrain forever.
But my mind is weak, and I have to ask,
Why couldn`t we be together*

.

*Now I`m old that love shines bright
And I still want you day and night.
But the time has come, and I do agree
That age at last has set me free.
Oh sweet sweet cake that time is here,
And my life is oh so clear
Together we will always be
Because now my teeth, are safe, beside me.*

RESCUE

Joyce Spalding

I could hear the bird screaming from inside the house and, as I hurried down the garden towards the bird feeders, it was easy to guess what had happened. The top had come off the narrow wire suet ball holder and a young starling had tried to go inside to retrieve the last tiny bit of suet. It was wedged inside with one wing coming out of the wire and it was screaming in terror.

I lifted the container down onto the bench. I didn't want to touch the bird but what choice did I have? I carefully put my hand on the wing. I could feel the fragile hollow bones under the feathers and under my hand. I tried to ease the wing back between the wires - trying to feel the natural bend of a folded wing. The bird still screamed in panic and I was in a state of panic myself. The feathers were so tiny but so stiff and if one of those bones broke my efforts to save it would be useless. Eventually I was able to get the wing inside.

Now I had to get the bird out. I put my hand inside the container around its body. The feathers were so soft, so silky and much softer than I had expected but I had never held a living bird before. I could feel the thrashing movements of the bird as it tried to get away from its prison and from me. Its chest seemed to move under my hand. Was I holding it too tight or was that normal? I didn't know. Then I had to try with my finger to hold its head still. The bone of its skull was so vulnerable under my touch. Gently I managed to ease it out from the fat ball container and as I opened my fingers to release it, it hopped quickly under the garden gate. Whether it survived or not I shall never know.

DRIFTING

Barry Seddon

Days full of drifting leaves the colours of fire. Nearly lunchtime. The girls, the lovely girls, many still in their summer dresses, would be joining him soon, strolling in twos and threes around the placid waters.

Swans were sailing there like yachts, admiring their own perfect reflections, preening, performing that bewitching arching of the neck, for all the world like cats lifting paws to wash behind their ears.

Malcolm Meredith sighed as he leaned back on the bench, relaxing in the unseasonably warm September air. People were already talking of an Indian Summer, though not many of them would know that the phrase had crossed to England from colonial India, where it meant misery for many and blessed coolness for the few who could afford to take to the hills. For goodness sake stop it Malcolm, you're not still a teacher!

He sighed peacefully again. So lucky, he was so lucky. Blessed, really, his life a comfortable round of walks, occasional visits to old friends, a meal out now and then, and the company of his three children and their own children -- when their busy lives in distant cities gave them time.

He loved those visits, particularly the maturing marvel of his seven grandchildren, three assured young men and four lissom young ladies, on whom he could spend some of his little-needed savings. Wasn't it unfair, the way young couples lacked money when they needed it, for mortgages, cars, ever-growing children and all the other cash gobblers? And when the children had flown the nest, the mortgage had been paid and a smaller car was enough, there was money to spare.

Yes, he was lucky. He had his health too and his hearing was keen enough to detect the arrival of the secretary girls. Here they came, long legs striding confidently, hips swaying just enough to swing their colourful dresses. Bright they were, as bright as the leaves. They lifted his heart.

Weather permitting; Malcolm strolled to the park nearly every day, often calling at the George and Dragon on his way home, for a leisurely pint of bitter. Many of the lunchtime girls knew him and said a bright hello, but today something lovely happened. Two of the young women sat and shared their break with him.

They introduced themselves -- Lily a diminutive strawberry blonde, Jane taller, a dark-haired foil to her friend. Both were slim, friendly and, in their early twenties, pictures of health. They had brought sandwiches and, as they ate, regaled him with tales of office intrigues, and romances.

Too soon however, their 40 minutes were up. They left him, with hopes of meeting again, joined the laughing brigade heading for the park gates, and were gone.

The day was still bright and warm, the swans as serene as ever, a shy little breeze swirling the kaleidoscope leaves. Still lovely, yes, but quiet with the girls gone, the girls in their summer dresses.

Malcolm made his way home more slowly than usual. In his mind's eye floated an image of Margaret, his wife, who had relaxed out of her life two years ago and quietly left him to mourn.

The memories were not so jagged now. There was still a wistful edge to them, but these days he remembered many more of the happy times, more rounded, less painful. And now, as ever, he was remembering the days when they had strolled in the park he had just left. When life was sun-filled and Margaret wore summer dresses just like his young lunchtime friends.

And his lady had been as pretty as any of them.

ODE TO A BUFFOON

alan Rick

Dear old Boris, we thee implore,

to go away and clown no more.

But if that effort be too great,

well - go away at any rate.

June 2016 – EU Brexit debate

A Lesson in Life.

Alan Rick

Behold the awestruck parents as they await the event that will change their lives in ways they could hardly imagine. The nurse turns to them with an impeccably professional smile. The parents collapse into unfeigned joy – for unto us a child is born. The newly arrived bursts into a noisy greeting, not understanding what all the ecstatic faces peering down at it are all about and the parents begin the mandatory billing and cooing that are an essential part of this event. Oohs and Aahs rent the air like soap bubbles that melt away, "He looks just like you", or like a distant cousin twice removed who is not here to defend himself. He/she is not just a blob with holes in it but a living exclaiming entity with the combined characteristics of its parents and a selection of the extended family.

Let us move forward to the age of 4 or 5 and now he cannot only walk and talk, but engage in near mortal combat with others in the street or in the playground, which he has now adopted as his own war zone. Yet he is still cute even though. During a football match, for which he has provided the ball he suddenly decides to take it home simply because he can. Reasons for an action are not required at this age, simply the ability to carry it out. Size triumphs over reason in all things.

The years roll by and the fond parents continue to enjoy the cute foibles of the little man as he stumbles from one day to the next always bringing a smile to the faces of his elders with his charming little eccentricities.

Comes the fateful day when the parents wake and discover to

their dismay that the cute little chap has turned into…a teenager.

It suddenly dawns on them that they have entered mine-strewn territory, that there are explosive times ahead which will stretch their patience beyond its limits. This is the time when rights are demanded, when freedom is displayed and when adults and their taste in just about everything are consigned to antiquity.

"Nobody understands me." "I'm just establishing my identity." This will be from some GCSE textbook on psychology he has read, as he storms up to his room and slams the door, to remain there at least until the next meal is ready.

"Do you adults really care about the environment? It's your generation that polluted it."

"Yes," replies the father, "We polluted it with your generation."

There is now an impasse broken by the offspring.

"I think this household should be run on democratic lines, with free exchange of opinions as to how it should be managed," comes the textbook reply.

The father has heard enough and, assuming an air of authority, requests his son to sit comfortably on the armchair to listen for once.

"Are you quite comfortable," he began. "Pay close attention because you are about to receive a lesson in life. First you have received an education paid for out of other people's taxes, second you are eating the food paid for by others and third you are living in a house that others have bought. For all these reasons I don't really think that that gives you much of a say in how the household should be run."

There is now a prolonged silence after which one or two things will happen; more stomping upstairs and slamming of doors, or a realisation that the benefits of submission are actually worth it.

We were tasked with reporting on our own disasters in the kitchen.

The concluding pages contain some of the amusing results.

KITCHEN CALAMITIES

SWit'CH ensemble

Mavis Confesses a Weakness.

My kitchen disaster would begin as soon as I walked into the kitchen. Even before I had started to cook the oven would cry "Oh no! I am going to get burnt again." The stove would get ready for plenty of spills and splashes. The pans would be dreading what would be put in them.

It all started long ago when I was a young girl not long married. Bakers were on strike and we were unable to buy bread from the shops so I decided to make my own. Mix yeast and sugar I had been told so I did. The problem was I didn't know how much of each to use. Leave in a warm place. This I did, leaving the mixture on the radiator and then going to bed.

Next day - OH MY GOD! What had happened? It looked as though we had been invaded in the night. The mess was down the radiator, over the floor and trying to escape under the back door.

Not put off, I mixed the dough and put it in the groaning oven. After some time, my bread looked cooked. WOW I thought as I struggled to lift it from the oven. It was heavy but it smelt lovely and it even looked like bread. It was brown and crusty. I couldn't wait for my husband to come home to praise me on my cooking skills.

I am sure I heard the table crack as I dropped the bread onto it. Cheese and butter ready I started to cut then to saw but the poor knife gave up and snapped in two. Laughing, my husband went and got his hacksaw. This was not a joke. Struggling to lift my masterpiece I dropped it into the bin. Most of the street must have felt the earth move as it hit the bottom.

Next was my homemade blackberry pie. I had even been to pick my own fruit. Pastry made, fruit washed. Plenty of it. Make it nice and juicy. Although no one had told me that I should have cooked the fruit first. Once again my pie looked good. Custard sieved - all ready. Then another broken knife.

Times went on. My children thought home-made soup was supposed to be watery and gravy was meant to have lumps. That the turkey at Christmas was supposed to taste of plastic as I always forgot to take the plastic bag out and pancakes were meant to look like scrambled eggs.

I have improved although it has taken me nearly fifty years to do so. My boys are all men now and each one of them learned to cook at a very early age. I bet now when they sit back after a good meal they say, "I enjoyed that - but it's not like my mother used to make - THANK GOD."

Cooking wasn't the way to a girl's heart for Alan.

Well here I was, a young fledgling newly flown from the parental nest and luxuriating in the thought of a flat of my own. Armed with the mandatory social accessory necessary to all young men at that time – a girlfriend – I pondered how to enjoy my new found freedom. What better that to impress her with a meal cooked and presented by my own fair hand – what girl would not be dazzled by the skill of a budding ***CORDON BLEU*** chef?

How much money would be saved by not taking her to a restaurant? Though vaunting male pride prevented me from mentioning this last prosaic fact; such mundane trivia was surely below the dignity of a creative artist.

Marjory sat on the sofa gazing with misty eyes as I set about the task of cooking. Cooking was a rather grandiose term for this operation which initially involved heating a tin of tomato soup in a saucepan. Meanwhile roast potatoes were cooking on a metal tray in the oven and the toaster was taking care of slices of bread. The old saying 'biting off more than you can chew' should have come to mind, or in this case 'cooking more that you can cook.'

But, drunk with the heady wine of success, I dismissed Marjory's anxious looks with the words "There is no problem."

Never let it be said that cooking is just a routine chore that lacks drama. This event was about to turn into an epic of Shakespearian proportions. I removed the soup tin from the saucepan and opened it. But where was the soup?

Marjorie pointed to the ceiling;

"It's up there. You're supposed to drill a hole in the tin before you boil it."

The ceiling was nicely decorated in red. A further search revealed that the potatoes' stay in the oven had been forgotten and they were now black and the size of marbles. There was passion during a heated discussion in which Marjorie displayed a linguistic range quite remarkable in a well brought up girl. The toast had suffered a similar fate to the potatoes.

"Never mind cooking the pork chops," she said with a withering look, "I'm going home".

Thus were the green shoots of romance cut down in their infancy - and it took two boxes of chocolates and some flowers to coax them into growing again.

Mary admits an imagination deficit

When it comes to cooking, I have no imagination. This is probably because I find the whole sequence of the matter boring. Don't get me wrong, I love good food, especially when it's served up before me - which is not very often, as invariably I do most of the cooking for the family.

"Mum's coming for tea tomorrow," my husband stated, "Why don't you try and do something different? She's not really a fan of your roasts or hotpot."

"You could always do it yourself!"

"Love you," he smiled and closed the door behind him.

The following day I bought some nice fresh salmon, garlic, herbs, new potatoes and garden peas.

"I'll show him who can cook!"

Everything was done to perfection, simple yet inviting. A lovely sauce from the cookery book gave it the finish of a professional. I smiled and left it in the warm oven while I changed. Thankfully she was running late because my warm oven was actually set on high! To say it was dry was an understatement! Quickly I put in some cod to poach. With no peas left I only had cauliflower and potatoes fit only for mashing. With the white sauce done I relaxed a little, hoping it would be alright. Carefully I dished it out and with fingers crossed, placed it before them. Then, I realised the white fish had broken apart and being alongside the cauliflower and mash and covered with the white sauce it looked an absolutely disgusting white mass of indescribable food.

Out of manners they started to eat. It was bland to the point of nothingness. I had to say something. There was no way I could let them think I was that bad a cook. They relaxed, and after the sweet which was absolutely gorgeous and a glass of good wine the meal became the subject of many jokes and innuendoes for a long time. It was, by default, the best night we have had.

Bill's experiments didn't always come off.

Experimentation is the precursor to kitchen catastrophes. The green shoots of my culinary imagination first sprouted when I grasped the kitchen responsibility for myself and the other four lads sharing a semi-detached house in Liverpool. "Nobody Died" is the only claim I have to success – big lads don't take on the guinea pig role willingly so I wasn't chancing my life with *cordon gris*.

It was a different story however when I married and our finances would not run to fancy gadgets. So it was that baking in our early marriage was often accomplished by correct mixing and aeration of cake ingredients through the application of a wooden spoon in the jaws of Messrs Black and Decker's finest. I'm sure the additional roughage provided by the sawdust falling from the well-used tool contributed to the healthy growth of our children.

Standard cook book recipes were seen as the starting/jumping off point from which to create an "interesting" meal. Deserts were the easiest course to enhance, expand and embellish. 'Traffic light rice pudding' was a well-received success by the kids and it only took the application of fruit juice and jams to enhance the colour in this basic treat.

But there were also failures. I'd seen somewhere that grated cheddar adds an extra dimension to apple crumble. I prepared the apples, weighed out the flour, lard, sugar and grated cheese, then mixed and cooked the crumble.

At his first spoonful, John's reaction was "It's awful". I chastised him for not being prepared to try something new and similarly the next child and subsequent siblings who pulled faces after sampling the first spoonful of the desert. My wife's grimace was accompanied by an accusing question,

"What have you put in it?"

That's when I thought it only fair to try it myself and show them they were being unadventurous and altogether too negative. This experiment had gone wrong.

Do you know that, if they are both in unmarked Tupperware containers on the shelf, salt and sugar look identical?

Barry's recipe blends fire and water.

Looking back, I can just about smile, but a kitchen catastrophe is not funny while it is happening. Anything but.

It was nearly midnight, silence in the empty house and a velvet darkness outside. I might have been the last person alive. Not much more to write. Time for a break -- a nice big mug of coffee and a dark chocolate digestive. I headed for the kitchen.

It's physically impossible to obey some swear words, but that should not deter the expletives' inventor. Mine were as explicit as ever, but the cause didn't go away. I had left my bacon and egg plates and cutlery soaking in very hot soapy water -- and forgotten them.

Now the water lay cold and greasy and so did the pots. Looking wouldn't wash them though. I sighed, reached down gingerly into the piranha-infested water, found the plug chain and tugged. The water started to drain away and I set the hot tap trickling to get hot.

I then realised that in my hurry to start writing, I'd left the top of the stove spotted with blobs of fat from the sizzling bacon. The rings themselves needed burning off as well. I turned all four to a very low setting and hurried off to the bathroom to answer a rather urgent call of nature.

Relief took longer than expected, but I should have crossed my legs and stayed in the kitchen. It was a disaster area. The sink plug had slipped back in. Fed by the trickling tap, the water had risen, run along the two drainers and poured a gentle Niagara over the edge, into the washing machine control panel, into two drawers full of tea-towels, then across the tiled floor, glinting with greasy rainbow patterns.

Cursing again, I had turned the tap off when I felt warmth on my back. Fire! The stove rings were glowing red and eye-watering smoke was rising from a cork mat which I hadn't noticed overhanging one of the rings. One edge was glowing bright red and would clearly be in flames at any moment.

Amazingly, my panic faded. I turned off the stove, grabbed the mat and dropped it into the sink where it sizzled to safety. Then, nursing blistered fingers, I opened the windows, made a cup of coffee, paddled across my newly-acquired pond and went to sit outside in the drizzle.

Anne recalls 'roughing it' in a caravan.

We boarded a Fieldsend's coach at 9.00am on a drizzly and miserable Saturday morning in August. We were bound for Rhyl. It was the second week of Manchester Wakes. I had booked a caravan advertised in the Manchester Evening News for six pounds. There were no reviews or illustrations indicating what we were letting ourselves in for.

To pay for the holiday we had used my then husband's two weeks' holiday pay, plus eight shillings family allowance.

We carried only one suitcase for all four of us. Its contents included an uncooked chicken, other essential food items, toiletries, towels and clothes for four of us. The girls were aged two and a half and thirteen months. The trolley for Mandy, our baby, would arrive tomorrow on the day trippers' coach.

The campsite looked forlorn and neglected. It was not of today's standards of streamline caravans, home from home.

Rain poured down relentlessly, dropping from the trees and forming huge puddles on the untidy tarmac. Uneven rows of ugly caravans filled the site.

One caravan stood out from the rest. It was not because of its aesthetic appeal, but from its sheer ugliness. It could be described as bottle green, tiny and its distinguishing feature was the fact that it had 'stable doors'! The newspaper description described it as 'sleeps four'. Two bunk beds pushed against one wall were evidence that at least two people could sleep, but what about the others?

It took a while before realisation struck. The tiny dining table had to be transformed into a double bed. There was no running water. Buckets had to be filled from a communal tap out at the other end of the field. There was no toilet or bathroom. Those facilities were even a further distance than the water.

Sunday morning heralded more heavy rain filled clouds. My husband set off for Rhyl to collect the trolley (now more commonly known as a buggy), taking our older child Wendy with him. Mandy was not yet able to walk. I placed her on the floor to play, lit the small Calor gas oven and put the chicken in to roast.

After some time, I opened the oven door to check on progress. Damn! There was no cooking process. The oven had failed to ignite.

I reached up, struck a match.

Whoosh!!! The chicken flew out of the oven. A trail of fire followed it. I grabbed Mandy, threw her outside onto the wet grass and turned round to see the door mat in flames. I flung that out. Fortunately, it missed my wailing baby. I grabbed the sweeping brush, also in flames and began beating the fire out.

By now a crowd had gathered and began to help. The drama was over.

My husband returned, looked at me and asked what the hell had I done to my face. I looked in the mirror. My face was sunburnt red. My eyelashes and eyebrows gone. The front of my hair singed and frizzed.

The chicken lay forlornly smouldering in the wet grass, so it was fish paste butties all round for lunch.

OTHER PUBLICATIONS BY SWiT'CH

My Life and Other Misadventure   ISBN 978-1-326-60665-7
By Alan Rick

A collection of humorous and poignant nostalgic reminiscences covering Alan's early school years in the war to national service in Egypt. Alan looks askance at the society of the day with a wry, knowing, smile.

A Write Good Read   ISBN 978-0-244-73623-1

Tales from Swinton and Salford; the Wigan train and around the world drawing on the experiences and interests of the group. Modern telecoms and IT feature, so do the Ten Commandments and seven dwarfs. Historical pieces range from the industrial revolution to individual childhood memories.

Peterloo People   ISBN 978-0-244-18472-8

A potpourri of passions gives the reader the chance to walk in those shoes to the peaceful protest, the actions on the day and shameful reaction afterwards. But the focus is not only on the victims; the perspectives of the authorities and militia are treated with sympathy and criticism in due turn – and there's even a wry tale of hope and salvation for a pariah in the guise of a government spy.

The Taste of Teardrops   ISBN 978-0-244-26569-4
A Novel by Judith Barrie.

A gripping psychological thriller set in a sleepy seaside town on The Solway Firth. It's 1981 and a young woman settles into her cosy new home believing that she had found peace and tranquillity after a painful marriage break-up.

But there are mysteries. Who is the woman upstairs? And who is the irresistibly attractive man who visits her? Susan is unaware of the nightmare of pain and deceit he will draw her into, driving her to the very edge of her sanity.

The Big Switch   ISBN : 9798644090433

A collection of short stories in large print format for readers with a visual impairment such as Macular Degeneration or Glaucoma.

'The Big Switch' is a compilation of extracts from some of the group's previously published works. Designed for easy reading.

Memories Unlocked   ISBN 9798570919617

These childhood reminiscences of localities now gone, holidays, school, nature notes, plane crashes, sex education and walking home after dancing form part of the mischief, mayhem and misadventures of our young lives. Drawn from the experiences of SWit'CH writers in their formative years.

Selected Memories   ISBN 9798598323212

This choice of writers' recollections taken from Memories Unlocked follows on from *The Big Switch*, which was produced for those with a visual impairment, with a font developed by RNIB.

The book is easy to handle. Big letters on low contrast paper make it an easy read and a 'page turner' in the literal sense.

A Pain in the Bum   ISBN: 9798590032099

Veronica Scotton

The author's words say it all "I was so very fortunate, not to have to face my cancer alone. Whenever I began to feel overwhelmed, the rock who is my husband was by my side. My children and grandchildren lifted my spirits by being positive about the whole thing and my siblings and friends with their humour, often black humour gave me the best medicine."

Printed in Great Britain
by Amazon